A Coffin for Santa Rosa

Dying of typhoid fever, Ingrid Bjorkman asks Gabriel Moonlight to bury her beside her late husband in Santa Rosa. Knowing he's an outlaw with a rope awaiting him in New Mexico, she makes him promise to hire a Pinkerton to escort the coffin. But Gabriel loves her too much to let anyone else handle the burial and accompanied by her rebellious teenage daughter, Raven, he takes the coffin to Ingrid's former farm where her husband is buried.

But the shadow of the rope looms over Gabriel. Faced with betrayal, can he escape with his life?

By the same author

Gun for Revenge
Packing Iron

A Coffin for Santa Rosa

STEVE HAYES

A Black Horse Western

ROBERT HALE · LONDON

© Steve Hayes 2009
First published in Great Britain 2009

ISBN 978-0-7090-8845-5

Robert Hale Limited
Clerkenwell House
Clerkenwell Green
London EC1R 0HT

www.halebooks.com

Typeset by
Derek Doyle & Associates, Shaw Heath
Printed and bound in Great Britain by
CPI Antony Rowe, Chippenham and Eastbourne

PROLOGUE

Ingrid Bjorkman was dying and there was nothing he could do about it.

Never in his life had he felt so helpless. Filled with grief and a mounting anger that was fueled by frustration, Gabriel Moonlight paced dejectedly in the dimly lit upstairs hallway outside her bedroom, silently begging God to save her life.

Nothing else stirred in the big three-story house that everyone in Old Calico called the Blackwood Mansion. Save for the monotonous plodding of Gabriel's boots on the Persian carpet the only other sound was the slow, sonorous tick-tock, tick-tock of the old grandfather clock downstairs.

Presently the bedroom door opened and Dr Guzman came out, black bag in hand, his plump normally-jovial face creased with dismay.

Gabriel looked hopefully at him.

Dr Guzman shook his head and expelled all his despair in one long depressed sigh. 'We're losing her, Gabe.'

Gabriel grasped the smaller man by his lapels and jerked him close. 'Doc . . . surely there's somethin' you can do?'

'Don't you think I would've done it if there were – for Ingrid and Tom Goodwin and Aileen Freidrick and all the other patients I've lost in the past two months?'

There was no denying that and Gabriel grudgingly let the doctor go. 'What if I took her to Sacramento or Frisco – is there a doctor there who could save her?'

'I'm afraid not. And even if there was, it wouldn't make a lick of difference. Poor woman's so weak from intestinal bleeding she wouldn't survive the train ride.'

Gabriel, wishing he could lash out at someone, gritted his teeth and said angrily: 'I will not let her die, Doc. Y'hear me? I will not.'

Dr Guzman gripped the tall, grim-faced gunman's shoulder. 'I'm sorry, Gabe. I've done all I can. Now all that's left is to make Ingrid's last days as comfortable as possible. Hopefully, in the near future we'll have medicines that will cure deadly fevers like typhoid, but for now—' His voice trailed off. And as if embarrassed by his inability to save the life of his patient he turned away from Gabriel, rolled down his shirt sleeves, donned his coat and hat and plodded sadly downstairs, out of the house.

Gabriel, overcome by rage and despair, stood there in the hall wondering why God was taking the woman he loved away from him. Was it to punish him for all the men he'd killed; all the wrong-doings he'd committed? Was there, as he'd often suspected, really a balance to life? Did evil truly begat evil? Had his father, Reverend Ambrose Moonlight, been right all along when he'd warned miners in the Colorado gold camps, riff-raff who fought and killed each other over a single nugget barely worth a round of drinks, that their sins would catch up to them – as in 'an eye for an eye'?

Gabriel doubted it. Retaliation was a human trait; surely God would not stoop to such a low, primitive level; especially when dealing with the life of a woman as good and kind and gentle as Ingrid.

The bedroom door opened again and this time her young daughter, Raven, stepped out. 'Momma wants to talk to you,' she said, eyes brimming with tears.

Gabriel bent low and kissed her on the forehead. He then entered the lamp-lit room and approached the bed. The feverish, fair-haired woman who looked up at him was so gaunt and pale, so colorless she could have been made of wax. He kneeled beside her, pressed his hand over hers and forced himself to smile.

'Doc says you're doin' better,' he heard himself say.

6

*She gave a weak nod and her cracked lips worked with great effort.
'Much better. . . . ' It was a voice he didn't recognize; a voice so thin and
faint he had to lean close to hear her. 'W-Want you to promise me
something.'*

'Anything.'

'Make sure I'm . . . buried next to . . . Sven—'

*'Buried? What're you talkin' about? You ain't goin' to die. You're
goin' to live another hundred years or more.'*

*Ingrid tried to smile but the effort was too much for her. She fell silent
for a few moments, as if gathering strength, then said: 'Want you to
promise me something else too—'*

'Name it.'

'You won't be the one who takes my coffin to New Mexico.'

'Ingrid—'

*'No. I want your word on it. Get Mr Jacobs or some other lawyer to go
. . . or hire a Pinkerton . . . anyone . . . but not you. You'll be killed and
. . . I don't want . . . that on my conscience—' Before he could reply her
eyes closed and she drifted off somewhere.*

Frustrated by his helplessness, Gabriel waited for her to come back.

*Finally, her eyes, red-rimmed but still cornflower blue, gazed up at
him. She managed a faint smile. It was the smile of a dying angel. Then
slowly, in an ever-weakening voice, she made him swear that he would
hire someone to accompany her coffin back to New Mexico, where, at her
former farm outside the little town of Santa Rosa, she would be buried
next to her late husband, Sven.*

*A little later, when Gabriel came out of the bedroom, he found Raven
waiting for him. Fighting back her tears, she asked him what her mother
wanted. 'Please, tell me,' she said when he hesitated. 'I have to know.'*

'Told me to make sure I buried her next to your father.'

Raven frowned, surprised and dismayed. 'Momma said that?'

Gabriel, deciding one lie was enough, kept silent.

*'But you can't. Momma knows that. You go back to Santa Rosa, or
any other place in New Mexico an' Mr Stadtlander will hang you.'*

7

'He won't know I'm there.'

' 'Course he will. Someone will tell him. That's why he doubled the price on your head. Everyone knows that. Minute folks see you they'll run straight to him, or worse . . . they'll shoot you for the reward!'

'Now don't go gettin' lathered up over nothin',' Gabriel said gently. 'I already give my word to your mother an' I don't intend to break it. What's more,' he added, 'I don't want you sayin' nothin' about this to her, you understand? She's fightin' for her life right now. Last thing she needs is somethin' else to worry about.'

Raven glared at him, her jaw thrust stubbornly out, lips compressed in a thin white line. 'Fine,' she said finally. 'You don't want me to say nothing, I won't. But I'm going with you.'

'Like hell you are.'

'Then I'll go alone. She's my mother an' I got every right to be there when she's buried.' Before he could argue further she stormed off down the hall and slammed into her bedroom.

Gabriel sighed and toed the floor with his boot, an unconscious trait he did when troubled or frustrated. Hell's fire, he thought. Just when he reckoned he'd turned the corner on life it had done what it had done so often in the past: reared up and bitten him.

CHAPTER ONE

It was mid-afternoon when the train pulled into Deming, New Mexico.

A small, dusty, sun-drenched town located thirty-odd miles north of the Mexican border, it was the county seat of Luna County and had sprung into prominence once the Atchison, Topeka and the Santa Fe completed its junction with the Southern Pacific in 1881. Named after Mary Deming Crocker, the wife of railroad magnate Charles Crocker, it had finally shed its bad reputation for harboring border riff-raff, gunmen and outlaws – not to mention frequent attacks by marauding Apaches – and now, ten years later, offered settlers a chance of peace and prosperity.

Among the arriving passengers was a tall, rangy, wide-shouldered gunman in an old campaign hat and a tan duster that hid the well-oiled Colt .45 holstered on his right hip. Taciturn and enigmatic, Gabriel Moonlight was a man whose outlaw life had honed him to a dangerous edge. Beneath his calm, quiet exterior lurked a dark side; and though slow to anger, when finally aroused his rage was as sudden and lethal as summer lightning. As a result lawmen in the southwest weren't anxious to cross his path and to a man wished he'd been gunned down like most of his contemporaries.

Ironically, despite his deadly reputation, Gabriel considered himself to be cordial and humorous. But few people understood his wry, laconic sense of humor and those who did weren't particularly amused by it. This in no way bothered him. He'd been on his own too long to give a damn about strangers' opinions. But loneliness never loses the final battle and over the years it had left its indelible mark on him, both emotionally and physically. One look at him showed that. Below unruly dark hair that was prematurely tinged with gray, his lean, rugged, tight-lipped face was etched with weary resignation. And his eyes, deep-set eyes that were strikingly pale blue, possessed a lethal glint that warned everyone not to crowd him.

Seated beside him on the train was his ward, Raven Bjorkman. A slim girl of fifteen with short, gleaming crow-black hair, she looked boyish in an old sun-faded denim shirt and frayed jeans tucked into Apache knee-high moccasins. She too had unusual eyes. Large and expressive, they shone like wet coal and were a window to her personality – a unique blend of defiance, intelligence and gritty determination.

Now, as the train slowly pulled into the station, Gabriel Moonlight looked out the window and searched the faces of the people gathered outside the depot and the adjoining Harvey House – a large, elegant, fifty-room hotel and restaurant with elaborate second-floor balconies, all constructed of imported Oregon redwood. He saw no one he knew. Nor could he spot any lawmen on the lookout for him; at least none wearing a tin star. Inwardly he sighed, relieved. He knew he couldn't relax – any second someone might recognize him and try to collect the 'alive-or-dead' reward – but maybe, for the time being at least, he'd caught a break. Picking up the carpetbag on the floor between his feet, he rose and motioned for Raven to follow him.

She obeyed without argument, unusual for her. Rebellious to a fault, she hated to be told what to do and was quick to express it, especially when it came to Gabriel whom she took a devilish delight in defying. But today, she was too worried about his safety to argue with him.

'What're we going to do first?' she asked as they stepped from the train. 'Get Momma's coffin or take care of Brandy?'

'Coffin,' replied Gabriel. Carpetbag in hand, he led her to the rear of the train where the conductor was standing by the open door of a boxcar.

'Mr Bjorkman?' When Gabriel nodded, the conductor handed him a release form. 'Sign here, please, sir.'

Gabriel signed as Ingrid's dead husband, 'Sven Bjorkman,' and returned the form to the conductor. 'Anythin' else?'

'No, sir. Soon as we've taken on water, I'll have some men take the coffin off and then get a ramp to unload your horse.'

'The girl will handle Brandy.'

Gabriel didn't offer any explanation but after a quick, testing look the conductor wisely decided not to question him. Instead, he suggested that while they waited they enjoy the refreshments served in the Harvey House.

Raven was more interested in the all-black Morgan stallion roped off from the coffin inside the boxcar. 'Mister,' she told the conductor, 'don't try to unload the horse without me. He's dirt mean.'

It was an order, not a request and the conductor wasn't happy about it. He acknowledged her with a terse nod, 'I'll pass that along to the wranglers, miss,' and stalked off.

'Reckon I rubbed him the wrong way,' Raven said.

Gabriel shrugged, unconcerned. 'Happens.'

Inside, the Harvey House was as finely appointed as any hotel or restaurant east of St Louis. The main dining room was equally magnificent. Service was impeccable and the menu offered guests the same fancy meals they were accustomed to eating in Boston, Chicago or New York.

Not wanting to risk being recognized, Gabriel led the awed, wide-eyed Raven past the dining room and grand staircase to a small L-shaped lunch counter that occupied a corner of an

11

outer room. The two waitresses, dressed in their traditional matronly black uniforms and full-length starched white aprons, were young, attractive and courteous. Because of these attributes and the quality of the food, the restaurant and the counter were always busy.

Gabriel and Raven found two vacant stools next to the wall, opposite the kitchen, and looked over the menu.

'Glad to see you're learnin', scout.'

Compliments were rare and usually couched in riddles. This one seemed harmless enough, but she eyed him suspiciously.

'Learning what?'

' 'Bout Brandy bein' dirt mean. Wasn't long ago you told me he was just feisty.'

'I haven't changed my mind. But "feisty" don't throw a scare into anybody. And I wanted to make sure no one fooled with him. That way folks won't get bit, like they did when we took him back to Old Calico. You want someone to get bit?' she demanded when he didn't answer.

'What I want,' Gabriel said, thumbing at the pie-case, 'is a piece of that there berry cobbler an' a cup of eatin'-house coffee. How about you?'

'Same, please.' Raven expected him to tell her that she was too young to drink coffee. When he didn't, she was disappointed. 'Don't you care if I have coffee?'

'Why should I? I'm not your mom.'

'No, but you are my dad. Well, sort of, and—'

'No, your father's dead, like your mother. I'm just lookin' after you, like I promised her, till you're old enough to take care of yourself.'

'Then by God look after me,' Raven said, peeved. 'Tell me I have to drink milk 'cause it's better for me.'

Gabriel sighed wearily. Taking out the makings, he rolled himself a smoke and flared a match to it. Staring moodily at the

12

blackened match, he muttered under his breath: 'On the prod . . . always on the prod.'

'What'd you say?'

'I said,' he grumbled, 'how many times I got to win you over, scout, 'fore you quit tryin' to buffalo me?'

'I don't know,' she said, happy now that she had his attention. 'Till I'm full-growed, most likely, or at least till you quit being so persnickety.'

While they were finishing their cobbler, a signature dessert of the Harvey House, Gabriel asked their waitress if she could recommend a 'reasonable' hotel. She thought a moment and then suggested he try the Commercial on Silver Avenue. It was reasonable *and* respectable.

'I'll be needin' a livery stable, too.'

'That's also on Silver Avenue, sir, next to the blacksmith's. Can't miss it. There's a windmill and a water tower in back of it. Of course,' added with a laugh, 'there's windmills everywhere for that matter or they wouldn't call this Windmill City. Will there be anything else, sir?'

Gabriel shook his head. Paying her for the meal, he left a generous tip and got up to leave. Raven immediately asked him where he was going.

'Talk to the hostler.'

'Wait,' she said, gulping down her milk, 'I'll go with you.'

'What about Brandy?'

'What about him?'

'Can't be in two places at once.'

'Dammit, neither can you.'

'Whoa. Don't be cussin' at me.'

'Sorry. But you said you were going to get the coffin off first.'

'Already off.' Gabriel jerked his thumb at the window.

Raven looked and saw two workmen wheeling a plain wooden coffin on a low flatbed cart into the shade beside the depot. She could also see two wranglers sliding a ramp up to the boxcar containing the stallion.

'How am I supposed to look after Momma's coffin and get Brandy off the train at the same time?' she demanded.

'You'll figure a way.' He opened the door for her and they went out into the blazing hot sun. 'All part of bein' responsible.'

Raven scowled. She was beginning to hate that word.

CHAPTER TWO

Passing a 'Welcome to Deming' sign that numbered the population at 1621, Gabriel turned up Silver Avenue, walked two blocks, crossed Spruce Street and entered the livery stable. There was no sign of the hostler. Hearing the clanging ring of steel pounding steel coming from next door, Gabriel left the stable and went into the blacksmith shop.

A big, slab-shouldered, beetle-browed man in a leather apron stood by the forge, hammering a glowing red-hot horseshoe into shape atop an anvil. He didn't notice Gabriel for a few moments; when he did, he doused the horseshoe in a bucket of water, causing a sizzling hiss, and nodded politely. 'Afternoon, mister. What can I do for you?'

'Need to buy a wagon an' a team.'

'Sorry. I can't help you.'

Gabriel nodded his thanks and turned to leave.

'How long you need it for, mister?'

'Long as it takes to carry a coffin from here to Santa Rosa an' back.'

'Three maybe four days, huh?'

' 'Bout.'

The blacksmith sized Gabriel up. He found the tall man's uncanny ice-blue eyes unnerving, but admired the integrity he saw shining in them and decided to trust him. 'Would you agree to leave a deposit if'n I rented you mine?'

'Have to see it first.'

'Help yourself.' The blacksmith pointed past the old windmill to the stable. Then picking up his tongs, he grabbed the horseshoe and plunged it into the fire.

Gabriel returned to the stable and saw an old freight wagon standing in one corner. It had seen better days but was still usable. He then checked out the two big rawboned horses tied up in the stalls. In contrast to the Morgan, both were docile and friendly and thrust their heads out to Gabriel so he could rub their soft velvety muzzles.

'Well?' the blacksmith said when Gabriel rejoined him.

'It'll do. How much per day not countin' tonight?'

'Fifteen.'

'Ten's my limit. An' I need you to stall and grain my horse for the night, too.'

The blacksmith wiped his nose on the back of his hairy, meaty forearm before nodding. 'That comes to forty dollars plus a hundred for the deposit – just in case you run into trouble an' don't come back.'

'What kind of trouble might that be, y'think?'

'That ain't for me to say, mister. I'm just sayin' in case.'

Gabriel eyed the big man suspiciously. 'Ever seen me before?'

'Not that I recall. But when it comes to faces, I got me a memory worse than a dead frog. Can ask my wife. Folks come in and out of here all the time an' I never remember 'em.'

'Think you'll remember me?'

'Mister, second you walk out that door, I won't only forget what you look like but I'll swear you weren't ever here.'

15

Satisfied, Gabriel reached inside his duster, revealing the much-used, black-gripped Peacemaker on his hip, and counted out the money from his money belt. 'Be obliged if you'd have the team hitched an' ready to go by sunup. Oh, an' I'll need drinkin' water for two.'

The blacksmith nodded and returned to his hammering.

At the station, two wranglers stood by the boxcar watching as Raven led Brandy down the ramp. The irascible black stallion gave her no trouble until he reached the platform. But as she started to lead him away, he suddenly whirled around and tried to cow-kick the closest wrangler.

'Don't mind him,' she said as both men jumped back. 'He's just funnin' with you. And you,' she told the Morgan, 'behave yourself!' She led Brandy to the hitch-rail alongside the depot and looped the reins around the bar. Then she re-entered the boxcar, reappearing a few moments later with Gabriel's saddle on her back.

'Here, let me give you a hand, miss.' The younger of the two wranglers, a short bandy-legged redhead with a knife scar whitening his tanned cheek, reached to take the saddle from Raven.

She stepped around him. 'Mister, the day I can't carry a saddle is the day I get me a rockin' chair.' Knees buckling under the weight, she carried the saddle to the hitch-rail, dropped it and caught her breath.

The two wranglers closed in on her. Though they were smiling there was something menacing about their lurking presence.

'Fine looking piece of horseflesh,' the old wrangler drawled. In spite of his grimy appearance he had a cultured southern accent and the saddle-worn pants tucked in his boots were Confederate gray. 'How much you reckon your Pa wants for him?'

'Brandy isn't for sale.'

'Oughtn't your Pa decide that?'

'He'd tell you the same,' Raven said. Suddenly, she felt threatened by the men and wished she wasn't alone. 'Brandy's not for sale. Not now. Not ever.'

The young wrangler with the scar thrust his face into Raven's. 'Mighty full of yourself for a young'un, ain't you?'

Raven tried to step back but found herself trapped against the tie-rail, 'You better leave me alone,' she said defiantly, 'or you'll be sorry.'

'Yeah? An' just how will I be sorry? You goin' to put me across your knee and give me a tannin'?'

'If she doesn't, mister, reckon I will.'

Both wranglers whirled around and saw Gabriel standing behind them. His tight-lipped smile was more frightening than any angry scowl.

'Go ahead,' said the young wrangler. He clenched his fists, ready to fight. 'See what it gets you.'

Gabriel's right hand shot out with startling quickness. Clamping his forefinger and middle finger on the young wrangler's nose, he twisted hard, first right, then left.

The young wrangler yelped and hopped around, trying to break free. Pain made his eyes water. And when Gabriel finally let him go, he cursed and went for his gun.

Again Gabriel's hand shot out, only this time it was balled into a fist. The blow struck the young wrangler on the chin. Eyes glazed, he dropped like a felled tree, unconscious before he hit the dirt.

Gabriel turned to the old wrangler. For a long, quiet moment the two men sized each other up. Then the older man smiled, easing the tension.

'I'm obliged to you, brother, for not killing him,' he drawled. 'Little Bill's a hothead an' oft-times acts without thinking, but he

17

doesn't mean any real harm by it.'

'Ignorance is a poor excuse,' Gabriel said coldly. 'Might be wise if you taught your friend some manners when he wakes up.'

'I'll be sure and do that, sir. I surely will.' The old wrangler tipped his hat to Raven. 'Hope you'll accept my apologies for Little Bill's behavior, sister.' When she didn't reply but continued to glare at him, he helped the still-groggy young wrangler to his feet and led him away.

'You all right?' Gabriel asked her.

Hoping he didn't notice she was shaking, Raven nodded. 'I could've handled 'em, you know. Don't think I couldn't.'

'Thought never crossed my mind, scout.'

Unable to tell if he was serious or needling her, she said: 'Did you get a wagon?'

'Yep. Talked to the Station Agent, too. Said we can leave the coffin here till mornin',' he indicated a tool shed beside the stationhouse.

Raven looked at the shed and then at the coffin. The pale pine wood reflected the yellow glare of the dying sun. Tears welled up in her big black eyes as she thought of her mother lying cold, stiff and lifeless inside the simple box and she turned away so Gabriel wouldn't see them.

'Think it'll be safe there?'

'Reckon so. Door's locked at night. But if you ain't happy about leavin' it, I'll get the wagon an' we'll see if there's an undertaker in town.'

'N-No . . . I'm sure it'll be all right.'

Admiring her grit, Gabriel left her rubbing the Morgan's proudly arched neck and entered the depot. Returning a few minutes later, he walked to the tie-rail, fastened their carpetbag to the horn and picked up his saddle.

Instantly the Morgan swung its head around and took a nip at him.

Gabriel jumped back, cursing, barely avoiding the stallion's teeth. He then slapped the Morgan in the head with his hat so that it faced front, and threw the saddle over its back. Brandy arched his rump, as if ready to buck.

'Try it,' Gabriel warned the horse. 'An' I swear by God's little acorns I'll sell you for glue moment we reach Santa Rosa.'

Man and horse glared at each other, neither willing to back down.

'Good-God-awmighty,' Raven grumbled, tears forgotten. 'You two are worse'n tomcats in breeding season. Ain't you never gonna get along?'

Reaching under the Morgan's belly, she grasped the dangling cinch strap, slipped it through the ring and pulled it tight. Next she untied the reins, handed them to Gabriel, waited for him to mount and then let him pull her up behind him.

They rode this way into town. People walking along the planked sidewalks or riding on passing buckboards gave them curious looks as they trotted by. But no one seemed to recognize Gabriel or be alarmed by his presence and after cursory glances they went on about their business.

Gabriel searched their faces, one hand tucked inside his duster ready to draw his Colt if anyone recognized him. When they didn't, he realized luck was still with him. But he still couldn't relax. Not even when they reached the Commercial Hotel without incident.

Dismounting, Gabriel went to help Raven down. But she ignored his outstretched hands and jumped off by herself. He smiled, amused by her independence, and looped the Morgan's reins over the hotel hitch-rail.

'Promise me something,' she said.

'Have to hear what it is first.'

'You won't make me take no bath.'

'What would I do that for?'

' 'Cause I'm a girl and girls are supposed to smell pretty.'

'No fear of that.'

'Fear of what?'

'Folks mistakin' you for a girl.'

From anyone else, Raven would have considered that a compliment. But the way Gabriel said it, irked her. 'Now who's on the prod?'

He chuckled, untied the carpetbag from the saddle horn and led her into the large, two-story, brick-faced hotel.

The lobby was clean, comfortably furnished and smelled of cigars. Navaho rugs added color to the hardwood floor, southwest landscapes adorned the walls and the north-side windows enabled guests to enjoy a view of the Harvey House, railroad tracks and majestic Cooke's Peak. It was cooler inside than out, primarily because of the big ceiling fan that swirled the air around and kept the flies from settling on the guests in the lobby. Some were talking, others smoking or reading newspapers, but all stopped what they were doing as Gabriel and Raven entered, their eyes following them to the front desk.

'Need a room for the night,' Gabriel told the clerk.

The short, balding, bespectacled clerk tucked his thumbs into his gray pinstriped vest and frowned disapprovingly at Raven. 'The boy,' he asked. 'Might he be a kin of yours, sir?'

'He's a she,' Gabriel said quietly. 'An' I'm her legal guardian.'

The clerk bristled. 'I'm afraid the hotel has strict rules about breeds, sir.'

'We'll need only one bed,' Gabriel said as if the clerk hadn't spoken. 'Floor's more to my likin'.'

'Perhaps you didn't hear me, sir. We don't allow half-bree—'

He broke off, alarmed, as Gabriel reached across the desk and grabbed him by the lapels of his suit, lifting him off his feet.

'Mister, we've come a far piece . . . all the way from Old Calico

20

in fact, just to bury her mother.' Gabriel paused, noticing as he did that everyone in the lobby was now staring in shocked silence. 'It's a journey that saddens the heart an' crushes the spirit. On top of that we're hot an' tired an' mighty close to irritable. So hand me the keys to our room an' I'll forget you're a pimply, sawed-off jackass an' not gut you from neck to gizzard.'

He released the startled clerk, the movement opening his duster to reveal the bone-handled skinning knife hanging from his belt. The clerk stumbled back, tripped over his feet and had to grasp the desk to steady himself. Eyes bugged with fear, he quickly grabbed a key from one of the pigeon holes and handed it to Gabriel.

'T-Two eighteen, sir. Top of the stairs and to your right.'

' 'Bliged,' said Gabriel, signing the register.

Raven, who had never heard Gabriel utter more than a few words at one time, recovered from her surprise and glared at the desk clerk.

'I'll need hot water for a bath,' she said gruffly. 'Lots of hot water. An' soap too. Par-fumed kind. That clear, mister?'

'V-Very clear, miss. I'll have it brought straight up.' Badly shaken, he watched as Gabriel, carpetbag in hand, guided Raven toward the stairs.

'Neck to gizzard?' she giggled as they climbed up to the second floor. 'Good-God-awmighty, when'd you start talking like Jim Bridger?'

' 'Bout the same time you started takin' baths,' Gabriel said. 'Now move along smartly, scout. I once wintered with an ol' griz' sow didn't smell as ripe as you.'

CHAPTER THREE

Later, while Raven was taking her bath, Gabriel lit a cigar, left the hotel, crossed the dirt, lamp-lit street and entered *Los Gatos*, a small cantina.

Inside, it was dark, dingy and reeked of chili and refried beans. Gabriel checked out the two cattlemen drinking at the bar, sensed they'd be no trouble and surveyed the rest of the dimly lit room. His gaze settled on a man playing solitaire at a rear table. The only light back there was what filtered out of the kitchen. It wasn't enough to read by and Gabriel was surprised that the man could see his cards. Suspicious, he tried to make out the man's face but it was hidden beneath the wide brim of his gray felt hat. It was not the everyday Stetson but like the hats worn by plantation owners in the Deep South. The rest of the man was in shadow.

Feeling a twinge of uneasiness, Gabriel decided to keep an eye on him. Ordering a bottle of rye, he took it and a glass to a corner table. As he sat with his back to the wall, he looked toward the rear and realized the man had left. Guessing he must have ducked out through the kitchen, Gabriel rose and went to the table. The cards lay as the man had left them; the game still in progress. Gabriel absently put an eight of spades on a nine of hearts and then stuck his head in the kitchen.

A lumpy, middle-aged Mexican woman in a grease-stained white dress was stirring a kettle of chili on the stove. Behind her, the back door was open. Gabriel hurried to it and looked out. The alley was quiet, dark and empty.

Returning to the woman, Gabriel asked her in Spanish if she knew the man who had just run out. Wiping the sweat from her brow with her beefy forearm, she shrugged fatly and shook her head.

'Ever seen him before, *señora?*'

Again the woman shook her head.

Thanking her, Gabriel returned to the bar and asked the balding, fat-faced Mexican barkeep if he knew who the card player was. The barkeep didn't. Nor did he remember what the man looked like. But he did remember that he was a *gringo*, a very small *gringo*, who smiled with his mouth but not with his eyes and wore a strange looking hat.

'A gambler, maybe?'

'It is possible, *señor.*'

One of the cattlemen at the bar turned to Gabriel. 'Don't mean to stick my nose in, mister, but the fella you're talkin' about was no gambler.'

'Go on.'

'Me'n my partner Cal, here, went over an' asked him if he'd like to play a few hands of stud. Fella didn't even have the courtesy to look up. Just went on playin' Klondike like we weren't standin' there. Made me plenty sore, I can tell you. But before I could call him on it, Cal pulled me away.'

'Lucky for you I did,' said the other cattleman, 'or you'd be full of holes.' He turned to Gabriel, adding: 'This *hombre* had two guns, tied low like a shootist. Real fancy jobs. Nickel-plated with shiny white grips – kind you see in a Wild West show.'

Gabriel felt another twinge of uneasiness. 'Happen to recall what color his hair was?'

'Sorry, friend. He never took off his hat.' The cattlemen went back to their whiskey and conversation.

Returning to his table, Gabriel poured himself a drink, gulped half of it down then sat there watching the door. He sensed trouble was approaching and under the table kept one hand on his Colt.

He didn't have long to wait. He'd barely finished his drink when Sheriff Cobb entered. The veteran lawman was unarmed but with him was a gangling young deputy holding a Colt 12-gauge side-by-side shotgun.

A short hard-bellied man, hatless, with iron-gray hair, a weathered, intelligent face and drooping gray mustaches, the sheriff motioned for the deputy to remain by the door and then confronted Gabriel.

'Mind if I sit down, Mr Jennings?'

Gabriel tensed. Anyone who called him that knew he was an outlaw. And if the person was a lawman, it could lead to a rope. For a moment he considered shooting the deputy before the deputy could shoot him; but remembering his obligation to Ingrid and Raven, he restrained himself and motioned for the sheriff to sit. The lawman obeyed, making sure his movements were slow and non-threatening. Gabriel, ready to slap leather at any instant, signaled to the barkeep to bring them another glass.

The barkeep obeyed.

Neither Gabriel nor the sheriff moved, even blinked, until the barkeep returned behind the bar. Then Sheriff Cobb poured himself a drink, raised the glass in silent toast and downed it.

'First thing I want to say, son, is I'm not lookin' for trouble.'

'Makes two of us.'

'Glad to hear that. Maybe now you can quit nursin' your iron.'

'Not till your deputy, there, lowers his thunder-gun.'

'Reasonable.' The sheriff nodded at the deputy, who lowered his side-by-side.

Gabriel brought his hand up and laid it beside his other hand on the table. The two men studied each other like wary Alpha wolves. Gradually the tension between them lessened, but it still crackled like high voltage.

Sheriff Cobb poured himself another shot, grimacing as the cheap whiskey burned his throat. ' 'Cording to Mr Dunbar, the station agent, you're here to bury kin.'

'Not here. Outside Santa Rosa.'

'Please accept my deepest condolences.'

Gabriel nodded his thanks but said nothing.

'That means you'll be movin' on in the morning?'

' 'Fore sunup – 'less you'n that scattergun got other plans.'

Sheriff Cobb smiled without humor. 'That's to make sure you leave, son, not stay.'

'So you ain't lookin' to collect the reward?'

'Money's no good if you're feet-up. And we both know you could put a hole in me 'fore that fool nephew of mine could pull the trigger.'

'Possible.'

'Possible – impossible – either way it's a risk I'm not anxious to take.'

'Not even for a thousand in gold?'

'Is that what the reward is now? Been so long since I've seen a poster I'd forgotten. But to answer your question, Mr Jennings, no – it's not worth the risk. I've got a little money stashed away and I'll be adding more to it shortly. I can only do that if I'm still sunny-side up. Besides, folks around here pay me to *keep* the peace, not rile things up.'

'That why you ain't packing?'

'I don't carry a gun, Mr Jennings, 'cause I got no need for it. Times are changing. Gunmen like yourself – and I don't mean this as an insult – your days are winding down. Pretty soon, Washington and maybe even state governments will pass laws forbiddin' a man to carry a sidearm.'

Gabriel found that hard to imagine, but kept his thoughts to himself. Downing his rye, he poured them both another. 'Anythin' else, Sheriff?'

'Matter of fact, yes.' Moving cautiously, hands always in sight, the sheriff pulled a piece of paper and a stubby pencil from his vest pocket and placed them before Gabriel. 'I'd like your John Henry. It's a hobby of mine,' he said as Gabriel looked puzzled. 'Collecting the names of famous shootists I've run into. Earp, Garrett, the Kid, Doc Holliday – I got 'em all.'

'An' you want to add mine to the list, that it?'

'I suppose it's a tad ghoulish,' the sheriff admitted. 'But I'm hangin' up my star soon and when I do, I intend to write my memoirs. According to this publisher I met, folks back East crave that sort of trash. And the more autographs and pictures the better. Says I'll make enough money to retire in style. Name's Cobb,' he added as Gabriel picked up the pencil. 'Andrew J. Cobb. With two b's.'

Gabriel licked the lead of the pencil stub and signed his name.

'Gabriel Moonlight?' Sheriff Cobb looked puzzled.

'That's my birth-given name.'

'What about Mesquite Jennings?'

'I stole that from a dime novel. I was always was on the prod back then an' it sounded like the kind of name an outlaw would have.'

The sheriff grunted. 'I'll be damned. Well, if you wouldn't mind, I'd appreciate it if you'd sign that name for me. After all,' he said when Gabriel didn't answer, 'you are still a wanted man, Mr Moonlight. So it wouldn't actually be a lie, would it?'

'Reckon not.' Gabriel scrawled Mesquite Jennings across the paper.

'Much obliged.' Sheriff Cobb tucked pencil and paper away and got to his feet. 'Figure on comin' back this way any time soon?'

'Hard to say.'

'Well, if you do, look me up. I'll buy you a drink before

puttin' you on the train.' He paused to let his words sink in. Then getting no response from Gabriel, he finished his drink, tipped his hat and started for the door.

'Sheriff—' Gabriel waited for the lawman to turn and look at him. 'My signature . . . is it worth more if I'm dead?'

'A lot more,' Sheriff Cobb said. 'But I'm a patient man, son, so no need to rush things on my account.' Chuckling, he walked out the door followed by the deputy.

Gabriel poured himself another drink, drank, and looked at his reflection in the mirror hanging behind the bar.

The man staring back at him looked weary but fearless.

Gabriel raised his glass in silent toast, drank, and left.

Once outside in the cooling dusk, he quickly stepped to the right of the bat-wing doors so that he wasn't silhouetted against the light inside the cantina.

He stood there a moment, insects whining about his ears, searching the faces of passing pedestrians, wagon drivers and horsemen to see if he recognized anyone. He didn't. Nor could he see anyone lurking among the false-fronted buildings across the street, or hiding on the rooftops, either. Could he be mistaken, he wondered. Could the card player be someone other than Latigo Rawlins, a deadly Texas gunman who was both a hired gun and a bounty hunter? What little description Gabriel had been given fitted Latigo. Admittedly, it fitted other people too. But if it wasn't Latigo, who was it and why had he taken off so suddenly? Didn't he want Gabriel to see him? Was he an outlaw himself? Did he mistake Gabriel for a lawman, and high-tailed it out of the cantina rather than face him?

Having more questions than answers, Gabriel decided to let things play out. Stepping off the boardwalk, he warily crossed the street and entered the Commercial Hotel.

Collecting his key at the front desk, he went up to his room and knocked on the door. 'It's me, scout – Gabe.'

Raven opened the door. 'Well?' she asked, stepping back so he could get a good look at her. 'What do you think?'

He frowned and pretended to be puzzled. 'Thought you were goin' to take a bath an' get all gussied up?'

'Very funny. Ha ha,' she said, punching him. 'Now quit your joshin' and tell me how I look?'

Gabriel studied her. She'd bathed, brushed her short shiny black hair so that it framed her face, cut her bangs so they no longer hung over her large dark eyes, put on her only dress – a church-going yellow gingham frock with white frilly cuffs – and street shoes. She also smelled of hotel soap, a fragrance not unlike lilacs after a rain.

'Prettier than a spring foal,' he said.

'Think folks will still mistake me for a boy?'

'I'll shoot the first daisy who does.'

Raven giggled, stepped close and hugged him.

'Will you take me out to dinner, Mr Moonlight, sir?'

'Be honored to, Miss Raven, ma'am.'

CHAPTER FOUR

They ate at the *Oro Fino*, a timbered, family-owned restaurant on Railroad Avenue opposite the Union Depot. The food was simple and wholesome, the portions huge, and the prices much lower than meals at the Harvey House or one of the hotels. Though packed with cattlemen, miners and railroad employees, Gabriel and Raven managed to get a table by one of the two windows facing the railroad tracks and the dark scrubland beyond.

They ate heartily, wolfing down steaks, mashed potatoes, gravy and greens that left their stomachs groaning but somehow still found room for homemade pecan pie. Gabriel then bought two Mexican-made cheroots and smoked one of them as they headed back to their hotel. Though it was dark, street lights lit their way and showed their reflections in store windows.

Raven stopped in front of one and made funny faces at herself.

Gabriel paused and watched her. Her antics made him chuckle. Encouraged, she danced around and then curtsied as if before an audience.

'Hear them, Gabe?' she said, cupping one hand behind her ear. 'Everyone in the theater's clapping and cheering. They love me.'

He wanted to say that he loved her too, that with her mother gone she was now the joy making his life worthwhile, but as usual he couldn't find the words. Angry at himself for not being able to express his emotions, he said curtly, 'C'mon . . . it's too cold to be monkeyin' around.'

It wasn't what she wanted to hear. All the happiness fled from her face. 'Oh, you,' she grumbled, falling in beside him. 'Why do you have to be such a grump?'

Her words cut deep. Stopping, he did the only thing he could think of to show he cared: he bear-hugged her, lifting her clear off her feet and twirling her around so that her legs swung out like Maypole ribbons.

'L-L-Leggo,' she gasped finally. 'I c-c-an't breathe.'

Gabriel quickly set her down and apologized.

'Don't be sorry,' Raven said. 'I love it when you hold me. Makes me feel all warm and happy inside, like I did when Dad was alive.'

He smiled, silently pleased, and offered her his hand. She grasped it and together they walked to the corner. A tumbleweed came bouncing up the street. They dodged it, laughing, and crossed over. The buildings were spaced farther apart now, exposing them to a cold wind blowing in off the desert. It tugged at Raven's hair, threatened to blow Gabriel's hat off and swirled dust around them. The lightweight wool coat her mother had bought her in Old Calico wasn't much protection. She shivered and cuddled close to him as they continued on.

'I'll be glad to get back to California, won't you? Least there it's warm most of the time.'

Before Gabriel could reply, a man stepped out from a dark doorway and confronted them, a pearl-handled, nickel-plated pistol in either hand. Telling Gabriel to raise his hands and warning him not to move, he added: 'So much as twitch an' I'll gun you down.'

'Do I know you, mister?'

'No, but I know you.' Under the brim of the little man's gray plantation hat his narrow-set eyes were rat-mean. 'You're Mesquite Jennings, the outlaw.'

'No, no, he's not,' Raven said quickly. 'He just looks like him. Everybody says that, don't they, Pa?'

'Shut up,' the little man snapped.

'Tell him, Pa,' Raven urged. 'Tell him who are. Tell him you're my father, Sven Bjorkman.'

'Hush,' Gabriel said, deadly soft.

'Pa-aa,' began Raven.

'I told you to shut it,' the little man said. He turned to Gabriel: 'I recognized you soon as you entered the cantina. Would've braced you then but I figured you might have partners in there.'

'So you hid in the dark like the yellow-gutted weasel you are,'

Gabriel taunted.

The little man grinned. 'Sticks an' stones, mister. Can insult me all you like, it don't fret me none. Catchin' you is like kissing a rainbow. I'll be famous. Folks will point at me an' say "Look, that's the man who caught Mesquite Jennings".' He thumbed the hammers back on both pistols. 'Now, drop your gunbelt. Easy,' he warned as Gabriel reached for his belt buckle. 'Reward says alive or dead.'

'Please, mister,' Raven begged. 'You're making a terrible mistake. If you don't believe me ask the station agent, Mr Dunbar. He'll tell you. We just came here from Old Calico to bury Momma and he's lookin' after the coffin. It's in the shed there,' she pointed toward the train depot.

For an infinitesimal moment the little man's eyes followed her finger – and in that moment Gabriel, gunbelt now unbuckled, lashed out with it. It struck the man across his face, the weight of the heavy Colt in the holster stunning him so that he staggered and fell to his knees. Gabriel quickly swung the belt back the other way, this time striking him on the temple. He went sprawling on his face.

Gabriel was on him instantly. Face black with rage he began pistol-whipping the unconscious little man.

Raven flung herself on Gabriel, both hands grasping his flailing wrist, begging him to stop. 'P-Please, please,' she cried out when he ignored her, 'No more, Gabe! Stop it. Please! You'll kill him!'

It took a few moments but finally Gabriel stopped. He stood there, chest heaving, eyes afire, hands trembling, until his rage gradually faded. Then with his toe he rolled the little man onto his back. Though inert and bleeding, he was still breathing.

'Reckon now you know why I didn't want to bring you,' Gabriel said. 'Low-down jaspers like him, they're hiding around every corner just waitin' for the chance to pick up their blood money. Been lucky so far. But luck can't last forever. Next time, who knows? Might be my last.'

'Don't say that! Don't ever say that!'

'Denyin' it won't change the truth. Won't change who I am, either. Why'd you stop me anyway?' he asked.

' 'Cause you might've killed him. Then you'd be a murderer.'

'Most folks think I'm that now.'

'I don't care what most folks think. You're no murderer. You may have shot men, even killed them, but they always had a gun in their hand, didn't they? Didn't they?' she repeated when he didn't answer.

'Reckon.'

'That's the difference.' She waited for him to buckle on his gunbelt before adding: 'I couldn't love you, Gabe, if you were a murderer. Momma couldn't have either.'

Gabriel shot her a sidelong glance then picked up the two shiny, pearl-handled six-guns, looked at them contemptuously and heaved them into the middle of Railroad Avenue.

'Know what?' Raven said. 'When I first saw this fella, I thought he was that gunman you don't like, the one who stopped at our farm to water his horse, remember? Man you said was so fast on the draw?'

'Latigo Rawlins.'

'That's him!'

'Me, too,' Gabriel admitted, 'till I saw his pistol grips weren't ivory.' He spat, disgustedly. 'Latigo's many things, most of 'em on the devil's list. But he's no pansy. He wouldn't be caught dead packin' pearl-handled iron.' Taking her hand, he led her along Silver Avenue to the Commercial Hotel.

CHAPTER FIVE

Gabriel stayed awake that night. While Raven slept in the bed, he sat in a chair, blanket draped around him, gun in hand, ready to shoot anyone who tried to break in.

Next morning, before the first rooster crowed, they loaded the coffin into the wagon and drove out of Deming.

The sun hadn't yet cleared the distant, silhouetted peaks of the Cooke's Range. In the gray light before dawn the desert looked bleak and desolate; unfriendly. A cold gusting wind out of Mexico cut through the passes in the Florida Mountains and came moaning across the scrub-covered wasteland, chilling their cheeks and blowing sand into their eyes, making them water.

Behind them the town grew distant, the man-made forest of water towers and windmills finally disappearing behind a graveyard of rocky outcrops. Soon there was nothing but them and the empty desert, the creak and rattle of the old wagon and the steady, rhythmic thudding of the horses' hoofs the only sounds disturbing their thoughts.

Never a talkative man, Gabriel was quieter than Boot Hill before his morning coffee. Today was no different. Mind switching back and forth from Ingrid to Latigo Rawlins, he remained quietly vigilant in case some other bounty hunter decided to try to bushwhack him for the reward.

Raven, seated on the wagon-box beside him, was used to his moody silence and left him alone. Coat collar pulled up around her ears, hands stuffed in her pockets, she closed her eyes and tried not to think about how much she missed her mother.

Occasionally, she turned her head to check on the Morgan

striding freely alongside the wagon. At first when she realized Gabriel wasn't going to tie Brandy to the wagon, she'd protested, arguing that something might scare the temperamental stallion, perhaps even chase him off into the desert where he could get lost. But she was talking to a deaf ear.

'My luck ain't that good,' Gabriel told her sourly, and refused to discuss the matter further.

Gradually the sun came up, streaking the mauve sky with pastel pinks and yellows. And with the sun came the relentless heat.

For the first six miles the trail followed the old Butterfield Stage Line route to Las Cruces. The ground was hard and rutted by years of stagecoach wheels, and the jolting ride soon made their buttocks sore. But neither man nor girl complained, preferring to bury themselves in their grief as they tried to understand why the woman they'd both loved in their own individual way had so suddenly and senselessly been snatched from them.

After two hours or so, Gabriel pulled off the trail and stopped in the shade of some rocks. Building a fire, he heated a pot of coffee, sliced up a hunk of bacon and fried the strips in a pan. Next he took his last six eggs from a padded cigar box and cracked them into the hot sputtering grease. He spooned the grease over them till the whites were crispy brown; then when they were cooked to his liking, he wiped the pan clean with three buttermilk biscuits that had been wrapped in a kerchief and shared the food with Raven.

She eyed the biscuits suspiciously. 'How long you been carrying 'em around?'

'No more'n a month.'

'Hah! You didn't buy 'em on the train so you must've brought them with you from Old Calico.'

'Either way, they won't break more'n a few teeth an' you got teeth to spare.'

'I intend on keeping 'em too, thank you.' Raven broke off a piece of biscuit, slipped it into her slingshot and fired at a nearby cactus. Her aim was true and a spiky limb broke off. 'Well, reckon now I don't have to worry about fillin' my pockets with stones.'

Gabriel ignored her and dunked a biscuit into his coffee. It took a few moments before the biscuit was soft enough to eat; then he slowly munched on it, savoring each morsel.

Curious, Raven did the same with her biscuit. It didn't crumble and fall into the coffee like soft biscuits did and tasted better than she expected.

'Well?'

'Tolerable,' she admitted.

He grinned inwardly, knowing how much it irked her to admit he was right, and went on eating as if she hadn't spoken. It pained him to talk so much, but he knew it was keeping her mind off her mother's death and that made it worth the effort. Trouble was he was running out of things to say.

Sopping up the last of the egg yolk with his last bite of biscuit, he chewed contentedly before finally swallowing it.

'Mm-mmm . . . nothin' better than the taste of buttermilk biscuits.'

'That's what you said about the berry pie I made you. Remember? When Momma invited you to dinner? Said it was the best tasting—' she broke off, the thought of her mother bringing tears to her eyes.

Hoping to cheer her up, Gabriel said: 'Folks say the Good Lord labored six days makin' the universe an' rested on the seventh. But I'm here to tell you it ain't so. On Sunday He created buttermilk biscuits.'

'That's sacrilegious.'

'Not accordin' to the Mescaleros.'

'What's Apaches got to do with it?'

'Some bucks were goin' to skin me alive once till I cooked up a batch. Liked 'em so much they made me a blood brother instead.'

'You are such a liar.'

'Make up your mind. First sacrilegious, now liar. You're a varyin' woman, scout.'

'And you talk too dang much,' she said, exasperated. 'I liked you a whole sight better when I first met you and you hardly ever spoke.'

'Had a bullet hole in me then,' he said without thinking.

The memory of how she and her mother had rescued him from the desert, where he lay almost dead, reminded her about the coffin in the wagon and again she got teary-eyed.

Angered by his slip, Gabriel forced himself to grin. 'Yessiree . . . buttermilk biscuits . . . way to a man's heart, if it's his heart you're after.'

'Not me,' Raven said.

'Don't aim on gettin' hitched, that it?'

'Nope. Never.'

'Wise decision.'

'Not 'cause nobody will want to marry me, if that's what you're thinking.'

'Did cross my mind.'

'Reason I'm not getting wedded is I'll be too busy gettin' rich.'

' 'Cording to that fancy-pants lawyer worked for your uncle, you're already rich.'

'Rich-er, then.' Her boyishly pretty face wrinkled into a frown as she visualized her future. 'Know what I'm going to do with my inheritance?'

'Mean after you finish your book learnin'?'

' 'Course! I promised Momma I'd go to school and I intend to keep my word.'

'Brains is the way.'

'What?'

'You sure weren't standin' behind the barn when they gave 'em out.'

She realized in his quirky, off-beat way he was complimenting her. It pleased her. But she had no intention of letting him know that.

'Be serious, will you?' she scolded. 'I'm talking about after I'm educated. After I finish school and I'm all growed up.'

'Ah-huh. Reckon I wasn't lookin' that far ahead.'

'Well, I am. I have to. My dad told me, to be successful you got to plan your future. Start young, he said. Set goals. Have ambition.'

Noticing that her tears had dried up, Gabriel kept silent.

'Anyway,' she continued, 'soon as I'm old enough I'm going to buy a big hotel on the waterfront in Sacramento or maybe even San Francisco. One with a saloon and a casino and my name painted on the front in big gold letters. Then everyone will know who I am. You wait and see. I'll be more famous than Lily Langtry.'

She waited for him to respond. But he seemed more interested in cleaning his nails with the point of his skinning knife.

'And you know what else,' she said, marveling how the stallion's coat gleamed like wet tar in the morning sun. 'I'm going to divide all my money in half and give one half to you.'

Hiding his surprise he sheathed the knife, took out a cigar, bit off the tip, struck a match on his heel and lit up. 'Why would you do that?'

' 'Cause then you'll be rich too and won't ever have to worry about being wanted by the law again or becoming one of them sorry-lookin' old-timers who spend their days sitting around, chewin' and spittin'.'

'That's mighty charitable of you.'

She searched his face but couldn't tell if he was serious or teasing.

'Truth is, scout, I never figured on bein' rich. Never figured on bein' a sorry-lookin' old-timer either. But I did figure on spending my sunset years chewin' and spittin'.'

'I reckon that last part's all right,' Raven said. 'Just so long as you use a spittoon, not my porch. Don't want any of my guests tracking tobacco juice into the lobby.'

'Seems reasonable. What's more, I appreciate you offering to take care of me when it comes time to put my teeth in a glass at night.'

She sensed beneath his teasing he was serious and felt embarrassed.

'No need to make a big fuss about it. *Jumpin' Judas*! I'm just trying to pay you back for looking after me now.'

'I appreciate that, too. Gives a fella peace of mind knowin' he won't be thrown to the wolves. Now,' Gabriel indicated the wagon, 'unless you got to go pee behind them rocks, climb aboard an' let's ride.'

After another butt-aching, spine-jarring hour in the sun they approached a high-walled canyon. Ahead, the trail split, one way leading to Las Cruces and the other southeast through the canyon toward the town of Santa Rosa.

Gabriel guided the team into the canyon. The sand was softer here. Noticing a crushed cigarette butt in one of several hoof prints they passed, he reined up and told Raven to tie Brandy to the wagon. Knowing he never did anything without a reason, she asked him why.

'Comin' into broomtail territory.'

'Really? How can you tell?'

He pointed to his nose.

'You can smell wild horses?'

'When the wind's right.'

She sniffed several times. 'Can't smell a dang thing.'

'It's a skill takes some gettin' used to.' Eyes shaded by the flat brim of his hat he glanced about them, searching for any glint of steel among the rocks above them. 'Most likely they'll avoid us. But I don't want to risk Brandy gettin' tore up by some jealous mustang tryin' to protect its mares.'

Raven sniffed again. But all she could smell was the sweat of the lathered horses pulling the wagon.

'Use the halter back there,' Gabriel added, thumbing behind them. 'An' try to get to it 'fore Christmas rolls around.'

Grudgingly, Raven climbed over the seat into the back of the wagon, picked up the rope halter and clucked her tongue at the Morgan. The stallion came trotting up. She slipped the halter over his head, tied a rope to it and knotted her end to a ring fastened to the side of the wagon.

Gabriel slapped the reins across the backs of the two big horses. Both threw their shoulders against the harness and plodded on without complaint.

Raven returned to the wagon-box. 'Someday will you teach me how to smell wild horses?'

Before he could answer he saw a rifle glinting between some rocks ahead. Instantly he threw himself sideways, knocking Raven from the seat.

As both went sprawling onto the ground they heard a rifle shot.

'Get under the wagon!' he barked.

His words were drowned out by gunfire. Bullets ricocheted off the wagon and kicked up little spurts of dust all around them.

Making sure Raven was unhurt, he crawled behind the nearest wheel, aimed at where he'd last seen the rifle glinting and fired two quick shots.

More return rifle fire pinned them down.

The shots came from different directions and Gabriel counted three maybe four men hiding in among the rocks ahead of them.

'Can you see who it is?' Raven hissed.

Gabriel shook his head.

'Why're they shooting at us? Think someone recognized you in Deming and told the sheriff?'

Instead of answering her, he took off his hat and tossed it to his right. Instantly, a hail of gunfire followed as the bushwhackers all fired together.

Gabriel took quick aim and fired twice.

Raven heard a scream, and even as the sound echoed off the canyon walls, she saw a small red-haired man tumble down from the rocks ahead.

'That's him!' she pointed. 'One of the wranglers at the station who asked if Brandy was for sale.'

'Reckon they decided stealing was cheaper than buyin',' Gabriel said. Reloading his Colt, he gave it to her. 'Keep 'em busy while I get my rifle.'

Before she could argue he moved to the rear of the wagon, pulled the lock-pins free and slowly lowered the tail-gate.

'Aim at their smoke,' he told her, and climbed into the wagon.

At once the men hiding in the rocks opened fire. Bullets chewed at the wood around Gabriel. A few hit the coffin, angering him.

Raven, both hands clasping the big heavy Colt, did as she was told and fired at the puffs of rifle smoke.

Gabriel, meanwhile, crawled alongside the coffin and grabbed the Winchester lying behind the seat. Levering a shell into the chamber, he fired round after round at the rocks where he'd last seen the bushwhackers.

All shooting stopped.

No one moved.

Time froze.

'Hey, you at the wagon,' a voice yelled. 'All we want is the horse. Turn him loose an' you can go on your way.'

Gabriel judged where the voice was coming from, looked in that direction and caught a glimpse of red shirt between some rocks. He rested the rifle atop the wagon and fired rapidly. The bullets ricocheted off the rocks in all directions, one of them nailing the owner of the red shirt.

There was a sudden, painful cry.

A gaunt dark-bearded man staggered to his feet, dropped his rifle and collapsed. His body came flip-flopping down from rock to rock and landed on the canyon floor.

Immediately, a prolonged hail of bullets pinned Gabriel down in the wagon. Unharmed but covered in splinters, he lay there until the shooting stopped.

'Scout, you OK?'

'Fine.' Raven raised her head and squinted at the rocky canyon walls. 'How many, y'think?'

'Two less'n before.'

Silence.

High overhead a soaring hawk screeched in the wind.

Presently, they heard horses galloping off.

'Don't move,' Gabriel warned her. 'Could be a trap.'

They waited anxiously for several minutes. Then he crawled to the rear, jumped off and dived under the wagon next to Raven.

No shots were fired.

'Reckon they're gone.'

'Momma was right,' Raven said after a pause. 'Trouble follows you around like a lonely shadow.'

'Don't dispute that.'

'Know what else she said?'

'Maybe you should keep it to yourself.'

'Said I should always listen to you, and could trust you with my life.'

'Let's hope it never comes to that.'

'It just did and you lied to me. Why?'

Gabriel, deciding it was safe, slid out from under the wagon.

Raven immediately crawled out and stood up beside him. 'I asked you a question, Gabe. Why'd you lie to me?'

'Figured you had enough on your mind.'

'In other words, you didn't think I could handle it?'

His tight-lipped silence told her she was right.

'Now who's varying? First you tell me I'm responsible an' next you won't trust me enough to tell me the truth.'

She was right. What could he say?

Angry, she stared him in the eye. 'Don't ever lie to me again, all right? Otherwise, I swear I'll never trust you. Ever.'

Gabriel looked at her, at her boyish innocent face, her big black eyes so full of grit and determination, her full-lipped mouth that smiled easily yet revealed her stubbornness, and knew she was the best thing that had ever happened to him.

'Got my word on it, scout.' He stuck out his hand.

Raven continued looking into his light-blue eyes for another moment, as if trying to decide if he meant what he said, and then shook hands.

Up till then she had held her emotions in check. But now, as if overwhelmed by the whole experience, her lower lip trembled.

'I sure could use a hug,' she said, fighting tears.

She didn't have to ask twice.

He hugged her like it was the last time he'd ever see her.

CHAPTER SIX

That night they made camp in a remote, sheltered gully.

While Gabriel built a fire Raven went off and killed a rabbit with her slingshot. They roasted it over the flames and ate it for supper. When they were finished, Raven threw the bones and carcass out in the desert for the scavengers, leaving Gabriel to water the horses.

When it came time to bed down, he hobbled the Morgan and built the fire up in case the bushwhackers returned and tried to jump them. He then took the first watch and told Raven he'd wake her in three hours.

'You won't forget, will you,' she said skeptically.

'Gave you my word I wouldn't lie to you again, didn't I?'

Raven nodded, satisfied. Kissing him on the cheek, she yawned, said goodnight and curled up in her blanket beside the fire.

Gabriel refilled his mug with coffee, fired a smoke and leaned back against his saddle to contemplate his future. Now that he had Raven to look after he could no longer go through life not caring what happened to him. He had to stay alive, no matter what, until she was old enough to look after herself. That meant they had to get Ingrid buried, return to Deming and board a train for California as fast as possible – all the time hoping that no more bounty hunters recognized him from the reward posters scattered throughout New Mexico, Texas and Arizona.

A coyote yip-yipped in the darkness, interrupting his thoughts.

Gabriel looked at Raven asleep in her blanket. Just the sight of her made him feel good. But it also reminded him of her mother, Ingrid, and that didn't feel so good.

Rising, he went to the wagon. The pine coffin looked pale and lonely in the flickering firelight. Sadly he placed his hand on it, the wood feeling damp to his touch, and thought about the dead woman inside. Fate had thrown them together under the most unlikely of circumstances and now he was responsible for her daughter.

At first he'd thought Raven would be a burden, a nuisance even, but in fact the very opposite was true: having her around not only gave him comfort but added purpose to his life and now he couldn't imagine being without her.

'You miss her, don't you?'

He turned and saw Raven sitting up, watching him from her blanket.

'What're you doin' awake?'

'Was having a nightmare. This big ol' black bear was chasing me and. . . . You do, don't you?' she repeated. 'Miss Momma, I mean?'

'More'n I reckoned on.'

'Me, too. Lots.'

Feeling her pain, Gabriel came and hunkered down beside her.

'It's too late now, I know,' she continued, 'but I wish I'd been nicer to her. Momma always loved me and treated me fairly – even when I didn't deserve it – and I never realized that until she . . . till it was too late.'

'Only natural. All part of bein' a young'un. When I was growin' up I never thought much of my pa—'

She wasn't listening. 'You don't know this, Gabe, but I used to hate Momma and be mean to her.'

Gabriel remembered Ingrid saying that she was having problems with Raven, but decided not to mention it. 'Must've thought you had a reason.'

'Sure – on account of how Dad got killed. I blamed Momma for it. Said if she hadn't made him take her into town to pick up her stupid birthday dress he'd ordered from St Louis, he wouldn't have been in Santa Rosa and accidentally gotten shot by them three drunken cowboys. 'Course it wasn't really Momma's fault. Deep down, I knew that all along. Fact is, Dad was the one who nagged her into going. I heard him. Heard her telling him she didn't mind waiting until another day, too. But it didn't matter. Not to me. I was so angry about Dad dying on me when he didn't have to ... that ... well, I had to blame someone.' Raven paused, tears coming, and then said: 'You think Momma knows I really loved her? Now that she's dead, I mean?'

Gabriel smiled and put his hand against Raven's cheek. 'Sure.'

'Not just saying that to make me feel better?'

'Nope. Your mom knows. She knew all along, in fact.'

'How you know that?'

'Told me so ... at the farm an' at your uncle's house in Old Calico. Said she was the luckiest woman alive. Said God had given her a fine husband who loved her an' treated her special, and a loving daughter who meant more to her than anythin' in the world.'

'Momma said that?'

'More'n once. So quit your worryin', OK? Get some rest. You have to spell me in a couple of hours.'

Nodding, Raven lay back and smiled at Gabriel. 'I love you,' she whispered. 'I know I say hateful things sometimes, things that make you madder than a spit-on hornet, but that doesn't mean I don't love you. I do. More than anyone else in the world. Never forget that.'

He smiled, and gently kissed her on the forehead. 'Go to sleep.'

She yawned sleepily, 'Hope that ol' bear don't come back,' closed her eyes and almost immediately drifted off.

Gabriel pulled the blanket up under her chin. He then stirred the fire, sending sparks shooting up into the cool darkness. Stretching the aches from his weary muscles, he sat down, leaned back against his saddle and began rolling a smoke.

Being a surrogate father, he realized, was more complicated than he'd expected.

CHAPTER SEVEN

A little more than a year ago, when Ingrid and Raven had moved west to Old Calico, theirs was the farthest farm from Santa Rosa – almost an hour's ride from the edge of town.

Now, as they crested Mimbres Hill and looked down the long slope that reached across the desert to the farm on which she'd been born, they saw three other small spreads had sprung up. Beyond that the framework of a fourth partially built house stood at the foot of the hill.

'Good-God-awmighty,' Raven said, whistling. 'Where'd all them folks spring from?'

'Easterners, most likely,' Gabriel said disgustedly. 'Ain't enough they cluttered up all the land east of St Louis; now, thanks to the railroad, they have to stampede out here an' crowd our territory, too. Progress!' he spat out the word, adding: 'Pretty soon there won't be a place left where a man can ride without bumping shadows.'

Raven chuckled. 'Now you sound like my Dad. He hated to be crowded. That's why he and Momma moved way out here,

46

even though she would have preferred to live in Santa Rosa or even Las Cruces.'

'I never met your father,' Gabriel said as he guided the wagon down the hill. 'But the more I hear 'bout him the more I wish I had.'

Twenty minutes later they reached the farm. The entire property was now fenced in and there was an arched gateway with a sign welcoming travelers.

Gabriel reined in the team and stared about him in surprise. Beside him, Raven couldn't believe her eyes either: the new owner, Lylo Willis, who'd once owned the telegraph office in Santa Rosa, had turned the farm into a way station.

The cabin was now a large two-story wood-frame house, painted gray with white trim. Wooden steps led up to a shady front porch with a fancy trellis from which hung a sign announcing: 'Hot Meals Available!' The old barn in which Gabriel had recovered from near death had been enlarged and turned into sleeping accommodations. Next to it were two outhouses with 'Ladies' and 'Gents' signs on the doors. And beside the well, a well in which Ingrid had once hidden him from the law, stood a modern windmill bearing a sign with big red letters offering travelers water: fifty cents per adult, twenty-five cents per child and one dollar per horse.

'Is that legal?' Raven asked, shocked.

'It's their well,' Gabriel said grimly. 'No law sayin' they can't charge for the use of it. But it sure ain't neighborly.'

'Well, I'm not paying for water. 'Specially water that used to be mine. And I'm gonna tell Mr Lylo Willis that right to his mean ol' face!'

'Caution's the way,' Gabriel warned softly.

But Raven had already jumped down from the wagon and was marching toward a tall, paunchy man with thinning dark hair

47

and banker's spectacles who was talking to a Mexican helper mending a fence.

Before she could reach him a short, pear-shaped woman wearing a green scarf over her gray hair and an apron tied around her enormous waist came waddling out of the house. Pausing on the porch, she was about to call to her husband, Lylo, when she spotted Raven and broke into a big smile.

'Why, goodness gracious me,' she exclaimed. 'I don't believe it. Is that really you, Raven?'

'Hello, Mrs Willis.' Raven stopped and smiled at the woman. 'Yeah, it's me all right.'

'Well, good heavens, child! You come over here and give me a big hug right this minute. Why, I never expected to see you again!'

Grudgingly, Raven went over and let Mrs Willis hug her.

'Here, let me look at you.' She stepped back and held Raven at arms length. 'My o' my, you're all growed up. And so pretty. Your ma must be so proud of you.' Mrs Willis looked at the wagon, frowning as she saw Gabriel instead of Ingrid holding the reins. 'Where is your ma, child?'

'She passed,' Raven said.

'Oh, no-o. You poor sweet lamb. When? What happened?'

'Fever took her.' Raven turned to Gabriel, still seated on the wagon box, her eyes asking him to explain for her.

'Ingrid died a few days ago,' he told Mrs Willis. 'In Old Calico, a mining town near Placerville.'

'I've heard of it. Out west in California, ain't it, Mr uh—?'

'Moonlight,' Gabriel said. He climbed down from the wagon and stood, towering over the women. 'It was typhoid . . . there was an outbreak. Had somethin' to do with the water gettin' contaminated after an earthquake. Ol' Doc Guzman did his best to control it, but things got out of hand an' by the time it'd run its course, a lot of good folks were dead.'

'That's why we're here,' Raven put in. 'So we can bury Momma next to my Dad.'

Mrs Willis frowned. Subtly, her sunny demeanor changed and she became uneasy. 'Lylo,' she called, waving to her husband. 'Get on over here. You need to hear this.'

Lylo Willis knew better than to argue with his wife. Leaving his helper to finish repairing the fence, he trotted up to her.

'Yes, dearest?'

'You remember Raven?'

'Why of course. What a delightful surprise. What brings you—?'

'Now don't get to jawing, mister,' his wife snapped. 'The poor child's lost her momma and she and Mr uh—'

'Moonlight,' Gabriel reminded.

'Moonlight, have come all the way from California to bury Ingrid next to her beloved husband.'

Lylo Willis looked at his wife as if he hadn't heard her correctly. But the scowl on her round, beefy, cherry-cheeked face told him he had – and, more importantly, that she expected him to solve the unmentioned problem.

'I'm very sorry for your loss,' he told Raven. 'And there's nothing I'd like more than to accommodate your Momma's wishes—'

'What's stoppin' you?' Gabriel interrupted.

'N-Nothing, nothing at all.' Lylo avoided his wife's glare and turned back to Raven. 'It's just . . . uhm . . . I didn't know Sven was buried here.'

'Over there,' Raven said, pointing. 'Behind the barn.'

'Really?' Lylo Willis removed his spectacles, pinched his nose as if he had a headache, replaced the steel-framed glasses and did his best to look puzzled. 'Don't remember seeing a marker when we were rebuilding.'

'Then I'll show you. C'mon.' Raven led him and Gabriel to the barn and on, around in back, where Lylo's 16-year-old son,

Cory, was chopping logs into kindling.

Surprised to see Raven, he lowered his axe and rubbed the sweat from his eyes. 'What're you doin' here? Thought you'n your ma had high-tailed it to Californee.'

'Shows you how much you know, don't it?' Raven said.

'Get on with your work, boy,' Lylo told Cory. 'Got a wagon-load of folks to cook for tonight and your ma's low on firewood.'

Raven, who'd been looking around, now frowned, confused. 'It was right here,' she indicated, 'where we're standing.'

'That's impossible,' Lylo said, uneasily. 'There was no marker here when we tore the old barn down. Isn't that right, son?'

'Sure is, Pa.' Cory kept his eyes lowered and went on chopping.

'You're wrong, both of you,' Raven said. 'You saw it, didn't you?' she said to Gabriel.

He nodded. 'I watched her mother place flowers on the grave. Only it wasn't here,' he said, pointing to his left, 'it was about ten, twelve feet over there – ground that's now buried under your barn.'

Raven's eyes became saucers. 'You're right, Gabe! Dang it, I didn't think of that. You built over my Dad's grave,' she said to Lylo Willis.

'That's absurd,' he exclaimed. 'Your father and I were old friends. I wouldn't dream of desecrating his last resting place like that.'

'Mister,' Gabriel said, deadly quiet, 'I don't give a hoot about what you'd dream of doin'. It's what you done that matters.'

Lylo reddened, indignantly. 'You calling me a liar, sir?'

'There's a coffin in that wagon,' Gabriel continued as if Lylo hadn't spoken, 'a coffin containing the body of a fine, gentle woman who's waitin' to join her husband. An' I'll be damned ten ways to Tucson if I'll let her rot in the sun while you spin the truth around.' He pulled his duster back to reveal the

Peacemaker on his hip. 'Now what'd you do with it, Mr Willis?'

'D-Do with what?'

'Sven Bjorkman's body? Did you dig it up an' bury it some place else or did you, in your greed to turn a fast dollar, just tear the marker down an' build right over your "old friend"?'

Lylo Willis, about to erupt, wilted under Gabriel's ice-blue stare.

'I'll take you to him,' he said. Then to his son: 'Tell your ma where I've gone.'

'Sure, Pa.' Cory buried his axe into a half-split log and walked past Raven.

She tripped him, sending him sprawling. 'Liar! Dirty little weasel!'

Cory jumped up and took an angry step toward Raven, then he saw the rage on Gabriel's face and stopped, turned and hurried off to the house.

Twenty minutes later, with the sun blazing down on them, Gabriel halted the wagon alongside a crude wooden cross poking out of a small pile of rocks at the edge of Lylo Willis' property.

The three of them climbed down.

'See,' Lylo said, indicating Sven's grave. 'I done right by him, like I told you. I didn't have to rebury him, you know. I could've – and most folks would've – just built right on top of him. But I didn't. I—'

Gabriel cut him off. 'Get movin', mister.'

'What do you mean?'

'Start walkin'.'

'In this heat?'

'Now.'

'B-But it's almost a mile to the house.'

'Mile – ten miles – don't much matter. I'm about to bury a

51

good woman and you, mister, ain't fit to be in her company. Now, git.'

Lylo Willis grudgingly took a few steps then turned and glared at them. 'You'll be sorry for this.'

'Keep jawin',' Raven warned him, 'and you're the one who'll be sorry.' Reaching into the wagon, she grabbed the Winchester laying beside two long-handled shovels and levered a shell into the chamber.

Lylo Willis paled, turned and hurried off.

'I should've shot him,' she grumbled to Gabriel.

'It's a thought crossed my mind, too,' he admitted.

'Yet you let him walk away?'

'Got to thinkin', a fella like him ain't worth the price of lead.'

CHAPTER EIGHT

Despite the broiling heat Gabriel wasted no time in digging up the coffin holding Raven's father, Sven. Next he insisted Raven choose the place where she wanted her parents buried. It took her a few minutes to find the right spot. But eventually she picked a shady area at the base of a nearby rocky outcrop and then together they dug a grave wide enough for the coffins to lay side by side. Raven then said a brief prayer asking God to take care of her folks and to arrange for them to 'meet again in heaven.'

As she and Gabriel concluded the prayer by murmuring 'Amen,' the Morgan seemed to sense Raven's sadness. He came up and nuzzled her with his soft black nose, making snuffling sounds as if trying to say he was sorry for her pain. She stroked his forehead, whispering softly to him.

Meanwhile, Gabriel filled in the grave and covered the fresh-dug dirt with rocks to prevent scavengers from digging up the bodies. Then throwing the shovels in the wagon he prepared to start back to Deming.

'Aren't we going to make a cross?' Raven asked.

'No point in that.'

'Then how am I going to remember where my folks are buried?'

Gabriel drew his Colt and fired three shots at the rocks directly behind the grave site. The bullets ricocheted, each one chipping off a piece of rock before whining aimlessly into the desert. Pointing at the three silvery streaks the lead had left on the stone, he said: 'Now you got a permanent marker. Not one that, come next spring, will get washed away by rainstorms or floods.'

She looked at him, big dark eyes shining with admiration. 'Reckon you weren't behind the barn, either.'

For once he was caught off-guard. 'Barn?'

'When they were givin' out brains.'

'Ahhh,' he said, pleased. 'So some things do sink in, huh?' Fondly tousling her hair, he climbed onto the wagon-box and picked up the reins. 'C'mon. Jump up. Want to get rollin' while there's still daylight left.'

After they had traveled west a few miles the trail narrowed and snaked through a natural gap in the low rock-strewn hills. Known as *Pasa duro de Piedra*, or Hard-Rock Pass, it was a perfect site for an ambush. Gabriel, remembering the bushwhackers, instinctively looked up at the rocky slopes looming on both sides of them. Everything looked normal and he wondered why his belly was knotted up – a sure sign of pending trouble.

Seeing his uneasiness Raven said: 'More broomtails?'

Gabriel ignored her sarcasm and kept his eyes peeled. They rounded a bend that curved between two giant boulders and there, confronting them, was a line of riders blocking the trail. Raven counted ten of them, all armed with rifles that were aimed at her and Gabriel.

'Gabe—!'

He'd already seen them. 'Easy does it,' he warned. 'Don't do anythin' foolish or sudden.' Reining up, he kept his right hand away from his Peacemaker and looked behind him.

Ten more armed riders appeared, blocking off their escape.

Facing front again, Gabriel wrapped the reins around the wagon-brake, rested his hands on his knees and waited for the inevitable.

'Who are they?' Raven whispered, 'rustlers or lawmen?'

'Neither,' Gabriel said as the riders slowly closed in on them. 'They're Double SS boys.'

'Mr Stadtlander's men? How'd he know we were here?'

'Lylo Willis told him, most likely.'

'That snake,' Raven said angrily. 'I knew I should've shot him.'

John Welters, the foreman of the Double SS, now rode out from riders and confronted Gabriel. 'I'll take your iron,' he said, extending his hand.

Then, when Gabriel didn't respond, 'We got orders to shoot if you don't cooperate – you'n anyone with you.'

'You'd fire on a girl?'

'Not on purpose.' Welters, an erect ex-cavalry man in blue denim whose sun-strained gray eyes were almost as pale as Gabriel's, turned and indicated the riders. 'But the boys know how deadly you are with that Colt and they ain't goin' to be too particular about who else gets hit once they start shootin'.'

'Let her ride on out,' Gabriel said, 'an' I'll surrender peaceably.'

'Can't do that. Mr Stadtlander said I was to bring in all—'

'It's OK, Gabe,' Raven said, rising. 'I don't mind keeping you company.' Calmly, she climbed into the rear of the wagon.

Gabriel, sensing she was up to something, slowly drew his Colt and handed it, butt first, to Welters.

'And the rifle.'

Gabriel reached behind him, picked up the Winchester and gave it to the foreman.

For a moment Welters and the riders relaxed, as if danger had passed.

In that moment Raven leaped from the wagon onto Brandy's back, kicked the startled Morgan into a gallop, and charged straight at the riders milling around behind them.

Caught off guard, they tried to close ranks. But they were too late. Raven and the stallion burst through them and were in the clear before the riders could even think of shooting her.

A few half-heartedly raised their rifles, but they were basically decent men and no one could pull the trigger.

'Too bad,' Welters said, watching Raven ride off into the desert. 'Out there, she's buzzard meat.' He turned back to Gabriel, adding, 'Boss has been waitin' a long time for this.'

'That makes two of us, John.' Gabriel took the makings out of his shirt pocket and began rolling a smoke.

CHAPTER NINE

Raven kept Brandy at a full gallop until she was several miles from the pass; then a quick look back told her she wasn't being pursued. Only then did she slow the Morgan to a walk so the powerful stallion could regain his wind.

Ahead and on both sides of them was empty, open wasteland dotted with cacti, mesquite, and greasewood. Much of it was monotonously flat. But here and there gullies and low rocky hills broke the landscape while in the distance mountain ranges made up the horizon. The sun was starting to sink below their glowing peaks, warning that night was approaching. But Raven, though alone and without food or water, wasn't concerned. She felt at home in the desert, having grown up here and spent much of life learning how to survive in the wilderness.

Most of her knowledge came from the Mescaleros. They had no equal when it came to existing in this vast, harsh terrain and, though she was unarmed but for her slingshot, she had no fear of going thirsty or hungry.

But she was afraid that Gabriel would be killed by Stadtlander. From what she'd overheard Gabriel telling her mother, and what little he'd told her himself, his former employer was a ruthless, powerful rancher who was determined to hang Gabriel for shooting his only son, Slade.

It didn't matter to Stadtlander that Slade had been a gutless, drunken bully hated by almost everyone in Santa Rosa; or that he and his worthless whiskey-sodden pals, the Iverson brothers, had raped and killed Gabriel's former girlfriend; or even that Slade had cowardly shot Gabriel in the back first, before Gabriel whirled and gunned him down. No, none of those things mattered: all that the ageing, crippled rancher cared about was seeing Gabriel, a man he'd once loved more than his son, dangling from a rope.

'Somehow I've got to save him,' Raven thought aloud as she guided the Morgan eastward. 'And I got to do it fast.'

Brandy pricked his ears at the sound of her voice then tossed his head, flared his nostrils and snorted as if ready to do battle.

Raven responded by rubbing the stallion's ears. At the same

time she desperately tried to think of how she could rescue Gabriel. Nothing came to her. And as she rode on, she became more and more despondent.

It was then she heard a screech high above her. Looking up, she saw a bald eagle drifting on the thermals. She'd seen bald eagles before, though not often, but on those occasions the huge black, white-headed birds were soaring over the Rio Grande Valley or winging toward the mountains.

This one seemed to be deliberately hovering above her. Reining up, she watched it for a few moments, wondering as she did what was causing the eagle to remain overhead.

Suddenly, the huge bird folded back its wings and dived toward her. Surprised, Raven watched it plummeting straight down, talons extended, its savage cry reaching her ears. It never dawned on her that she might be the target. She knew golden and bald eagles snatched lambs and piglets from farms and on rare occasions were known to go after small dogs, but never a grown human being. Yet, even as she kept her gaze fixed on the eagle, it continued to dive toward her. In seconds, she realized, it would be upon her; and though she couldn't believe it, when it still kept coming she was forced to accept that she was its prey.

At the last instant, just before the eagle attacked her, Raven slid off the Morgan and ducked behind some rocks.

The eagle flew past her, screeching, and landed atop a nearby piñon tree.

For several moments girl and eagle stared at each other.

Raven, having never seen an eagle or any other bird for that matter behave this way, wondered why it was acting so strangely. It was almost as if it were trying to attract her attention. She knew that was impossible. Birds didn't have that kind of reasoning. Or did they? Come to think of it, she'd often heard strange tales of how animals and humans communicated with one another told around Apache camp-fires.

A loud whinny from Brandy interrupted her thoughts. The Morgan, in an effort to protect her, angrily charged the piñon tree. Though he couldn't reach the perched eagle, the stallion reared up, snorting with rage.

Unconcerned, the eagle suddenly launched itself into the air, circled once overhead and then flew off.

Raven emerged from behind the rocks. Still puzzled, she gazed after the eagle. She realized it was heading toward the Mescalero reservation. Triggered by the thought, she suddenly remembered Almighty Sky, the tribal shaman famous for his legendary shape-shifter abilities. Was the eagle really Almighty Sky, she wondered, or was it just a coincidence? And if the bird wasn't the wily old medicine man, had he used his powers to make it attack her so she'd remember him and know she wasn't alone?

She couldn't decide. But Almighty Sky had always been friendly toward her and her folks, and having no one else to turn to and with time running out on Gabriel, Raven swung up onto the Morgan's back and rode in the direction of the reservation.

CHAPTER TEN

Stillman J. Stadtlander's home sat atop a grassy knoll overlooking the Rio Grande Valley. It was a fancy three-storey mansion with ornately carved windows and a Roman-styled portico shading the front door. Built upon the site of the original single-story ranch-house, the mansion was a tribute to its owner's colossal ego and powerful influence throughout New Mexico.

Now, as sunset cast eerie shadows over the mansion and its outer buildings and corrals, Stadtlander sat on the porch, hunched over in his wheelchair, watching his riders escorting the wagon up the grassy incline toward him. As they drew closer his gaze fixated on the driver, a man he'd grown to hate with such intensity it drained all other emotion from him. Motioning to the Mexican servant beside him to hand him his crutches, Stadtlander gritted his teeth against the agony that every movement sent knifing through his arthritis-ravaged body and dragged himself to his feet.

Pain made him dizzy and he swayed momentarily. But when the servant went to help him, the old rancher cursed him so vehemently the young man cringed as if struck.

'Goddammit, I can stand on my own!' Pain struck again and this time Stadtlander winced and had to fight down a gasp. Glaring at Gabriel, still some distance from him, the rancher's leathery, jut-jawed face contorted with rage. 'I'd sooner die,' he told the servant, 'than give that ungrateful, murderin' bastard the pleasure of seeing me trapped in a wheelchair!'

His words were drowned out by the noise of the horses' hoofs and the creaking and rattling of the old wagon pulling up in front of him.

Ordering Gabriel to get down, Welters turned to Stadtlander. 'What do you want me to do with him, boss?'

'Beat him,' Stadtlander said flatly.

Welters cocked a reproachful eyebrow at the irascible old rancher. 'Sure that's what you really want, Mr Stadtlander?'

'You questionin' me, John?'

'No, sir. Just makin' sure I heard right.'

'You heard right. Now you'n the boys get to it. Beat the sonofabitch till he can't even crawl and then lock him in the barn. Come daylight,' he said speaking to Gabriel, 'I'm personally going to put a noose around your neck an' watch you kick an' dance until you choke to death.'

Gabriel eyed the enraged, crippled old man as if he pitied him. 'I'll do my best to make sure you ain't cheated,' he said grimly.

They were the last words he would speak that night. Welters clenched both hands together in a single fist and clubbed Gabriel on the back of the neck. Stunned, Gabriel dropped to his knees. The foreman grudgingly signaled to the ranch hands and they closed in and began punching and kicking Gabriel until he lay senseless and bleeding in the dirt.

CHAPTER ELEVEN

It was almost dark when Raven reached the Mescalero reservation. She hadn't been there in over a year; in fact not since the day she'd begged Almighty Sky to let the Sacred One, Lolotea – a beautiful young blind girl with premature white hair who possessed spiritual healing powers – leave the reservation and come to the Bjorkman farm to save Gabriel's life.

Now, as Raven rode into the main village, she was appalled at the squalid conditions. The dome-shaped hogans all needed re-thatching, trash and discarded whiskey bottles lay scattered everywhere, and every man, woman and child she passed looked listless and half-starved.

She rode on, attracting little attention from the downtrodden Apaches gathered about their fires, and finally reined up outside Almighty Sky's hogan. A small circle of blanket-shrouded elders sat silently in front of it. Motionless, they stared impassively into the flames. Raven smelled a pungent odor and knew they had been drinking fermented mescal.

There was no sign of Almighty Sky.

Wondering where the old shaman was, Raven dismounted. At once, two women in buckskin ceremonial dresses with red ribbons and sprigs of sage woven into their braids approached her. The younger of the two, a spindly girl no more than sixteen, carried an armful of blankets. The other woman, who was wrinkled enough to be a hundred, held a flaming torch in her withered left hand.

'It is good you have come,' she said, speaking Mescalero. 'The Wise One has been waiting for you.'

Raven frowned, puzzled. 'How could he be waiting for me when I had no idea I was coming here myself?'

'It is written,' the old woman said simply. 'Now, hurry. You must cleanse yourself before you hear the Wise One's message.'

Even more puzzled, Raven allowed herself to be led to a small pool. The clear water was encircled by smooth sandstone rocks on which were painted ceremonial symbols and strange-looking serpents, eagles, and an Inca-styled dragon identical to one she'd seen in a picture book. She and her folks had been friendly with the Mescaleros for years and Raven was no stranger to the reservation, but she'd never seen these rock paintings before and wondered why she was being permitted to see them now.

After they had undressed her, the women insisted she stand in the shallow pool while they bathed her and washed her hair with soap made from a yucca root. The water was numbingly cold and Raven couldn't stop shivering. At last, the women led her ashore and dried her with blankets scented with mint. They then wrapped her in a large red blanket, fastened it about her throat with a woodpecker's feather and led her back to Almighty Sky's hogan. There, they draped her clothes on a bush near the Morgan and told her she was now ready to see the Wise One.

'Go inside, child,' the older woman said. 'Meet your future.'

Raven stood there a moment, nervously wondering what this was all about. The elders were no longer seated about the fire, which had burned down to embers; but smoke curling out of the smoke-hole in the roof of the hogan indicated they were gathered inside.

Here goes nothing, she thought and ducked through the low doorway.

Inside, it was dark save for a small fire burning amid a circle of stones in the center of the hogan. Almighty Sky and the same elders were seated around the fire. But unlike outside all the men were now naked save for G-strings. None of them looked up as she entered; instead, they stared fixedly at an unusually tall peyote cactus growing in a clay pot positioned in front of the old shaman. The floor of the hogan had been swept clean and sage sprinkled over it. Raven vaguely remembered her father telling her that the Mescaleros considered sage to be a friend of the peyote. She hadn't understood what he meant then, but now seeing it scattered on the ground she guessed this was what he was referring to. Next to the pot lay a deerskin pouch tied at the neck by a red string.

Almighty Sky sat with his back to the west. There was a place left for Raven in the circle that was south of the doorway. The old shaman, lidded eyes downcast, motioned for her to be seated.

Raven obeyed. But embarrassed to be naked before all these men, she kept the red blanket pulled tightly about her.

Almighty Sky nodded at one of the elders. He began beating a small drum. At the same time he chanted softly, all the while staring into the fire.

The old shaman untied the string around the pouch, opened it and reached inside with his left hand. He then began passing out handfuls of peyote buttons. He passed them to his right, which was to the south, and when everyone had two handfuls he served himself and then replaced the pouch next to the pot.

In the flickering firelight Raven saw that some of her buttons were green with tufts on them, the others dry. The green ones were the size of a silver dollar, the dried buttons no bigger than a small pebble.

The elder stopped beating the drum.

Almighty Sky now looked at Raven for the first time. 'We, The People, are honored by your visit, *Ish-kay-nay*,' he said, using the Apache term for boy or one who is indifferent to marriage or, in Raven's case, tomboy. 'Too many moons have passed since we last shared words.'

'This is true, Wise One. But it was not because I did not want to see you, but because my mother and I moved a great distance away.'

'This was told to me in a vision,' Almighty Sky said. 'I am happy for your new life. But I am much saddened by the loss of *Nah-tanh.*'

Raven frowned, surprised. 'You heard about Momma's death?' she said, forgetting it was rude to ask him a direct question.

'I hear many things, *Ish-kay-nay*. This particular sadness was whispered to me by the wind.'

'While you were soaring above me?'

Almighty Sky didn't respond.

'I ask you this, Wise One, because I followed a bald eagle here. And I am wondering if those were his eyes watching out for me or yours.'

Almighty Sky frowned, his face a thousand wrinkles. 'Many strange mysteries occur when I stare into the fire, *Ish-kay-nay*. Not all of them have answers.' Putting a peyote button into his mouth, he chewed it slowly and then swallowed it, his expression never changing. At once, the elders began eating their buttons, one after another.

Raven, who'd heard from her father how horribly bitter peyote tasted, especially the green tufted buttons, hesitated before eating one.

Immediately, a strange thing happened: the fire crackled and blazed as if stirred and in her mind she heard her name called. The voice belonged to Almighty Sky. It came from far off yet each word was as distinct as if he were talking into her ear. Raven looked across the fire at the old shaman. His eyes were closed; his lips sealed. He was chewing stoically, rhythmically, and in the flickering firelight his gaunt, wrinkled face was etched by eerie shadows.

Suddenly his eyes opened. They focused on her. She felt herself drawn into them. Trust in me, they said. And you will come to no harm.

Almighty Sky's assurance was all she needed. Popping a button in her mouth, she began to chew. Expecting the taste to be unbearable, she was surprised to find the peyote was tasteless as sawdust. Her mind wandered. She thought of various different tastes, all of which she enjoyed, each of those tastes becoming what she tasted: blueberry pie, lemonade, Gabriel's buttermilk biscuits – even the licorice-tasting *Black Jack* chewing gum that her now-dead Uncle Reece had given her – all flooded her senses.

Swallowing the peyote, Raven began chewing another button and then another, all the time enjoying the variety of pleasing tastes that filled her mouth. Meanwhile, Almighty Sky's voice continued talking to her. No woman, he explained, Apache or Pale Eyes, had ever been allowed to sit at a Peyote Ceremony. She was the first. The Sacred One, Lolotea, whose soul had recently joined the Great Spirit, had appeared to him in a vision and told him to invite Raven. She had chosen Raven, she explained, because she was pure at heart – and because of this

64

the poisonous cactus would not taste bitter or unpleasant, or, more importantly, make her ill.

Raven felt her mind expanding. Everything became hazy. The room swam about her. She began to hallucinate. Suddenly, like a shower of exploding fireworks, a kaleidoscope of colors dazzled her eyes. She felt weightless, as if she were floating. Looking down, she saw herself seated in the circle with the elders. She watched herself chewing the peyote buttons. The buttons changed color and size then disappeared. The fire beckoned to her and she swooped down like an eagle and became engulfed in the flames. She expected to be burned. But the fire was her friend and she remained unharmed. She heard herself laughing. Thanking the fire for not burning her, she flew back to her seat in the circle.

Opposite, across the fire, Almighty Sky fed himself a handful of peyote buttons and instantly shape-shifted into a mountain lion, then an owl, then a rattlesnake with two heads. Raven watched as one head swallowed the other. Now a white woodpecker flew out of the remaining snake's mouth. The little bird flew around inside the hogan, shaking tiny, soft feathers from its wings. The feathers floated down like falling snow but never landed, turning the air into a silent, swirling snowstorm.

Raven looked up and saw Lolotea's angelic face smiling at her among the drifting snowflakes. The Sacred One spoke without sound. The feathers were sucked into her mouth until only one feather remained. It floated down and landed on Raven's face, balancing on her upturned nose. She grasped it and held it tightly in her hand.

Waving it like a magic wand, she felt herself levitate and fly away. Suddenly, large wooden doors opened in front of her. She couldn't see herself but she knew, as in a dream, she had entered a barn. A man lay sprawled on some straw. He was tied up, his face bruised and bloodied from a beating. Faceless ranch-hands entered carrying a rope. One threw the rope over the rafters so that a noose dangled. The other men picked up the beaten man, looped the rope around his neck and hoisted him up until his feet were off the ground. He hung there, kicking and choking.

Raven realized the dying man was Gabriel. She screamed and ran forward, grasping his legs and trying to support him so that he could breathe. But the men dragged her away and held her, helpless. The men now had faces. She recognized them as the riders who had jumped them on the trail. She turned her head away. But the foreman grasped her face and forced her to watch Gabriel die.

She fainted.

Everything went dark. Silent.

CHAPTER TWELVE

She awoke, choking. Someone was pouring liquid down her throat. Raven opened her eyes and saw Almighty Sky bent over her, holding a gourd containing water. A silver moon sat on his shoulder. Feeling groggy, she blinked, wondering if he was a hallucination. His wrinkled, weathered face remained before her. But when he moved closer the moon slipped off his shoulder and returned to the starry sky. She looked about her and realized they were now standing outside the hogan.

'Drink, *Ish-kay-nay*,' Almighty Sky said. 'You will feel better.'

She drank. For a few moments nothing happened. Then her stomach twitched. Suddenly, like a volcano erupting, she vomited. Almighty Sky gave her more water. She vomited again. Then her stomach settled, her head cleared and, as he'd told her, she felt better. Realizing she was still naked under the red blanket, she collected her clothes from the bush, ducked behind the Morgan, dressed quickly and returned beside the old shaman.

'Come,' he told her. 'It is time to make good smoke together.' Before she could protest, he led her over to the elders. Huddled in blankets, their bronze impassive faces showing no effects from the peyote, they sat smoking large fat cigarettes. They puffed slowly, holding the cigarettes pinched between finger and thumb so that the tobacco packed inside the loosely-wrapped corn husks would not fall out.

'Wait,' Raven said as Almighty Sky went to sit down. 'There is something I must tell you. While I was chewing peyote I had this vision.'

'Tonight there were many visions, my daughter. Yours will keep till morning.'

'No, it won't! It can't wait! You don't understand. It's important!'

'Tell me then, if you must.'

'I saw my friend, Gabe – Gabriel. You remember him, don't you – the tall Pale Eyes whose life was saved by the Sacred One?'

'Yes, *Ish-kay-nay*, I remember. He was a man who spoke straight.'

'Well, right now he's in danger. He . . . he's tied up in a barn and we got to get him out of there!' Raven quickly explained what had happened to Gabriel and how in her vision she'd seen Stadtlander's men hang him. 'He could be dead already for all I know, but there's a chance he isn't an' if you'll help me we can—'

'We?'

'Your warriors and me.'

Almighty Sky wrinkled his withered lips, showing shrunken toothless gums, and gestured about him. 'Look around you, *Ish-kay-nay*. Do you see any warriors?'

'No, but—'

'All you see is a defeated people.'

'My father,' Raven said stubbornly, 'told me there was no such thing as defeat. He said defeat was only a state of mind.'

'Your father was a brave man and a true friend of the Apache. I will not quarrel with his words.'

'That mean you'll help me?'

The old shaman sadly shook his head. 'I only wish I could, my daughter.' He closed his eyes and was silent so long she wondered if he'd fallen asleep. Finally, he looked at her and said: 'It is no secret that we Apaches call ourselves *Nde*, The People. We have lived here as warriors for a thousand moons. Like our ancestors, we roamed free, hunting where we wanted, fearing no one, living in harmony with the Earth God. But no more. The day of the warrior has ended. Forever. We have become farmers who cannot farm, beggars with no food to beg for, prisoners in our own land, our once-proud spirit broken by Agency laws, starvation, and firewater.'

Raven had never heard Almighty Sky speak so passionately. Her heart ached for him. But she desperately needed his help. 'What you say is true, Wise One. But surely there are still men among you who can ride an' fire a rifle?'

'We have no rifles, *Ish-kay-nay*. The White Eyes' law forbids us to arm ourselves. As for ponies, those that have not been killed for meat to feed the hungry are so feeble they cannot be ridden.' His tone softened and for a brief moment he rested his fragile, wrinkled hand on her shoulder. 'Go now, my daughter. There is nothing here for you. Nothing here for anyone. Soon the desert sand will blow over this land, covering everything, leaving no trace that The People were ever here. It is written.' He sat down, picked up the makings from a basket and began rolling a smoke.

Raven angrily stamped her foot. 'If you won't help me, Wise One, then why did you bring me here? Why did you send me a vision?'

Almighty Sky looked up at her, his watery red-rimmed eyes filled with compassion. 'I have but shown you the mountain, *Ish-kay-nay*. How you climb it is up to you.' He took a stick from the fire and touched the glowing end to his cigarette. Puffed contentedly.

Raven stood there, dejected, hoping against hope that Almighty Sky would change his mind.

He didn't. Frustrated, she had no choice but to mount up and sadly ride away.

Gabriel tried to open his eyes. His lids wouldn't respond. His head pounded so hard he thought it might explode. Overwhelmed by dizziness, he lapsed back into oblivion.

He had been slipping in and out of consciousness ever since the beating. Now, several hours later, he came around again and this time he forced himself to stay awake. Every part of him ached. He again tried to open his eyes. It took great effort, but finally he managed it and blinked a few times. His eyelids felt stiff and puffy. He realized they were swollen from punches. But he kept blinking and gradually his focus cleared.

Looking about him, he saw he was sitting on the urine-soaked floor of Stadtlander's barn, roped to a post with his hands tied behind him. Every breath he took caused a stabbing pain in his side. Guessing his ribs were broken, or bruised, he glanced up and saw a sliver of pale gray sky showing through a crack in the roof. Dawn was coming, he realized. It reminded him of Stadtlander's threat to hang him at daylight. He had to get free – and fast. Gritting his teeth, he ignored the pain and strained against the rope. When that didn't work, he tried to wriggle his hands free. It was hopeless. The rope binding his wrists would not budge.

So, he thought sardonically. This was how his life was going to play out: dangling ingloriously at the end of his former employer's rope! Hardly the death he'd hoped for – yet, he had to admit, probably justifiable. He had killed for the man and now the man was going to kill him.

How ironic.

How disappointing. Now he wouldn't be able to keep his word to Ingrid and protect her daughter while she grew up. The thought of failing her chewed at him. He licked his split lips, the saliva making them sting. He didn't mind dying so much – for a gunman or an outlaw death was always a heartbeat away. He'd learned to accept that. But to not be able to watch Raven, the one joy in his life, grow into the fiery, high-spirited, successful woman he knew she'd be – well, that was something he'd die regretting!

CHAPTER THIRTEEN

Once off the reservation, Raven wearily rode in the direction of Stillman J. Stadtlander's ranch. Stretching north, east and west from the Mexican border, it covered tens of thousands of acres, including a large portion of the fertile Rio Grande Valley.

The closest boundary line was only five miles away, the ranch-house another mile after that. Raven still had no idea how to rescue Gabriel, but she knew she had to think of something fast. Stadtlander would most likely wait for daylight before hanging Gabriel and one look at the sky told her that dawn was no more than an hour away. Desperate, she kicked the Morgan into a mile-consuming gait.

They crossed a flat, arid valley sheltered on the north and east by mountains. The south lay open all the way to the Mexico, which was farther than she could see. Ahead, craggy outcrops loomed up like dark sentinels guarding the wasteland. In the east the gray, cloudy sky was turning pale and tinted with lavender, signaling the approach of dawn. Presently, a fresh breeze sprang up bringing her campfire smells. Exhausted and hoping a cup of coffee would keep her awake, she slowed the weary Morgan to a walk and looked around for signs of a camp.

Smoke spiraled up from behind nearby rocks. She steered Brandy in that direction. Clumps of Palo Verde and mesquite rose up in front of her. Riding between them, she skirted the rocks and saw several men gathered around a fire. Behind them grazed a herd of horses.

Gabriel had taught her that it was dangerous to ride in on night camps without first announcing herself, some jumpy cowboy might instinctively fire off a few rounds. So, reining up a short distance from the fire, she was about to call out when a rider appeared out of the darkness.

'Hold it right there,' he growled.

Raven obeyed, instantly regretting that she hadn't ridden on.

The rider nudged his horse closer, his rifle glinting in the moonlight. His Stetson was battered and soiled, and by his unkempt beard and grimy clothes she guessed he was a drifter. As he got close enough to see her face, he gave a surprised grunt. 'Well, I'll be a Judas goat! You ain't nothin' but a sprout. What're you doin' way out here, girlie? You lost?'

'No-I-ain't-lost.'

' 'Course you're lost,' the rider said, mockingly. 'Why else would you be ridin' around in the middle of the night?'

'I'm on my way to visit someone.'

'Yeah? Who?'

'My grandpa – Mr Stillman Stadtlander.'

She'd only intended to impress him enough to make him let her go, but by his expression and low whistle she realized she'd

71

done much more than that.

'Halleluiah, boys!' he yelled to the others. 'Reckon we just hit pay dirt!' Before Raven could stop him, he grasped the Morgan's bridle and led her into camp.

The cruel-eyed, bearded faces that stared at her as she approached the fire all belonged to border trash. Raven tried to hide her fear, but inside she went numb. These were brutal, lawless misfits who killed, robbed and raped without reason or conscience. Drifters, gunmen, rustlers – she couldn't have been in more danger if she'd ridden into Geronimo's camp twenty years ago.

Meanwhile, the rider was whooping it up. 'Know who her grampa is, fellas, Stillman J. Stadtlander hisself.'

The rustlers crowded around her, peering, grinning, jostling each other just to get a closer look at her.

'Well, well, if this isn't justice,' one said. 'Y'all remember me, sister?'

Raven looked at the gaunt, gray-bearded, tobacco-stained face grinning up at her and realized it was the older of the two wranglers at the train station in Deming who'd wanted to know if Brandy was for sale.

'Reckon you're not feeling so feisty now, huh?' He spat, rolled his chew to his other cheek, and turned to the others. 'She's the little gal I told y'all about – one who was with her pa, a gunman, looked like, who shot McClory and Little Bill in Black Water Canyon.'

The rustlers glared at Raven. Realizing they blamed her for the death of their companions, she panicked and tried to back the Morgan up. But the rustlers quickly grabbed her legs and pulled her off the stallion's back.

Enraged, Brandy reared up, lashing out with his forelegs, scattering everyone around him. Free to escape, the Morgan instead charged the men holding Raven. They jumped aside, one of them dragging her with him.

'Run! Run!' she yelled to Brandy.

But the stallion wouldn't abandon her. Again he charged her captors. Again they dived aside. As Brandy wheeled, ready to charge again, several of the rustlers threw ropes over the stallion's head while others lassoed his legs, jerking the Morgan off its feet.

'Stop it!' Raven screamed. 'Leave him be!' She struggled to break loose, but her captors quickly overpowered her.

'You better let me go!' she hissed at them. 'Right now! Or my grandpa will hang every last one of you!'

The rustlers howled.

'Not one of us here ain't got a rope waitin' for him,' a wiry, long-legged drifter said. He jerked his thumb at the stolen horses behind him. 'As for your high and mighty grampa, reckon he and his boys are already out combing the hills for his stock.'

'If you let me go,' Raven said desperately, 'I promise I won't tell him about the horses. I won't even say I saw you.'

'That's mighty considerate of you,' the old wrangler drawled. 'But turning you loose wouldn't be conscionable. Pretty little flower like you, all alone out here in the desert, who knows what might happen?'

'I say we forget the horses,' the long-legged drifter said. 'I say we go brace Stadtlander an' see how much he's willin' to pay to get his precious granddaughter back safe an' sound.'

The old wrangler chuckled. 'Ordinarily I'd play along with you, Luke. But I already rounded up a buyer for them broncs. So unless y'all feel like pissing away money you already risked your necks for, I say drive them to Valley Verde like we planned.' He waited for the chorus of 'ayes' to die down before adding: 'I'll catch up with y'all later. Then once Mr Eldon pays us off, we'll figure out a plan how to get ransom money out of Ol' Man Stadtlander.'

The rustlers nodded in agreement. Mounting, they began herding the stolen horses together.

Meanwhile, the old wrangler dragged Raven over to the fire, made her sit down and bound her ankles.

'How you going to take me to my grandpa,' she demanded sullenly, 'if you let those men steal my horse?'

The old wrangler grinned, showing broken teeth. 'First thing you ought to know, sister, is Stillman Stadtlander doesn't have a granddaughter. Doesn't have a wife or children or next of kin, either. He's the last tree standing. So quit feeding me fish stories an' tell me where your pa is?'

'I ain't telling you anything.' Raven turned her head away and angrily watched as the rustlers rode off with the stolen horses. Two riders had ropes around Brandy's neck and were forcing the half-choked Morgan to run between them.

'Suit yourself.' The old wrangler picked up a discarded bottle of rye and drained the last few drops. Then wiping his lips on the sleeve of his old fringed jacket, he flung the bottle away and hunkered down in front of Raven. 'But I'm not long on patience, sister. So unless y'all want me to use ways to make you talk, you better answer my question.'

He thrust his face in hers. He reeked of sweat, liquor and trail dirt, making her recoil.

'Go ahead,' she said defiantly. 'Do what you want. I still won't tell you nothing.'

The old wrangler sighed, as if what he was about to do went against his nature. Then reaching behind his neck, he pulled a foot-long Arkansas Toothpick from under his shirt and poked the tip of the blade into the fire.

'Despite what you think,' he said, watching the steel turn red then white, 'I'm not a mean cuss. But Little Bill was kinfolk. And before I grow much older I aim to settle the score with your pa.' He paused, took the now-glowing-white blade from the fire and held it close to Raven's face. 'For the last time, little sister, tell me where he is.'

Raven felt the heat from the blade and shrank back fearfully. 'He's not my pa,' she blurted. 'That's the truth,' she said as the old wrangler inched the knife closer. 'I swear. Can ask anyone in Santa Rosa. They'll tell you. My father's dead. Was shot down in the street a while back.'

'Then who's this fellow?'

'Just a man my momma liked. Me'n him come out here by train from Old Calico. Momma caught a fever and passed a few days back. Made him promise to bury her next to my father. You saw the coffin. It was in the wagon while you were shooting at us.' She paused, a plan now forming in her head. 'Soon as Momma was in the ground I ran away from him. I hate him much as you do. Maybe more.'

'And why would that be?'

' 'Cause he's flat-out mean. Was always whipping and cussin' me behind Momma's back, making me do stuff for him.'

The old wrangler, sensing she was telling the truth, lowered the knife. 'When you ran off from him, where was that?'

'At Mr Stadtlander's ranch. He and Gabe – that's the man's name, Gabriel Moonlight – are old pals. If you want,' she added, seeing she had him hooked, 'I could take you there. We'd have to ride double and get there before daylight so no one sees us sneaking around. But if we find a place to hide, like maybe in the barn, when Gabe comes in to saddle up, you could take him down.'

The old wrangler mulled over her suggestion. Raven could see he found it appealing, but daunting, and knew she had to convince him.

'I ain't saying it'll be easy. But you got no choice. Before I ran off, Gabe told me he was going back to California soon as he left the ranch, so this'll be your only chance to get even with him for killin' your kin.'

'By God, I'll do it,' the old wrangler said. Then, sobered by the thought, he grasped Raven by both shoulders and pulled her face within an inch of his. 'Better not be telling me tall tales, sister, or I swear I'll cut your gullet out.' He pressed the point of the still-warm blade against her neck, making her gulp with fear.

CHAPTER FOURTEEN

Valley Verde occupied the center of a deep volcanic basin that was sheltered on three sides by steep, flat-topped cliffs shaped like a horseshoe. Green and peaceful, with a shallow creek running through the south end, it was home to a variety of wild creatures. This included a herd of wild mustangs led by a rare 'leopard' Appaloosa, an all-white horse sprinkled with blotchy, pinkish-brown spots that was known locally as *El Tigre*.

For several years the ranchers had tried to catch the white stallion. But it was cunning as well as uniquely beautiful, and they'd always come up empty-handed. One reason was *El Tigre* never grazed with the herd, instead preferring to watch protectively over them from atop one of the mesas. There, like a sentinel carved out of white marble, the canny stallion could survey both the herd and the entire basin in relative safety.

It was there today, shrouded by an early morning mist, as the rustlers drove their stolen horses into the south end of the valley. Nickering, *El Tigre* pawed angrily at the dirt and then charged down the narrow, steeply sloping trail that descended toward the herd.

Within minutes it reached the valley floor and galloped up to the wild mustangs. Its warning squeal alerted them that danger was close, and they were already in full flight when the stallion caught up with them. Nipping at the stragglers' flanks to make them run faster *El Tigre* herded the broomtails away from the rustlers.

There was a narrow pass leading out of the north end of the basin. Just wide enough for a horse to squeeze through, the entrance was concealed by dense brush and rocks. Few of the ranchers knew the pass existed, but it was known by the white stallion and was another reason why neither *El Tigre* nor the herd had been caught. To the cowboys chasing them, the mustangs always seemed to disappear into thin air, leaving behind a cloud of dust kicked up by their hoofs.

El Tigre used the pass now, leading the broomtails into the natural split in the rocky mesa and on, out the other side, into the open desert.

Earlier, when the rustlers entered the basin, they had been too busy driving the stolen horses to the creek to notice the mustangs. Now, as the herd waded into the shallow water to drink, the men dismounted, some kneeling to quench their own thirst, others splashing water over their faces or filling their canteens. According to the old wrangler, the buyer, a rancher who bought horses for the Army – buying cheap and selling at exorbitant prices – wasn't due until mid-morning; so, after building a fire, the rustlers sat around drinking coffee and smoking and bragging about all the whores they were going to bed once they got their share of the money.

Knowing that the Morgan was worth more than any of the other horses, the two riders in charge of the stallion kept their ropes around his neck while he drank. And when he was finished, they hemmed him in with their horses and tried to force him ashore.

That's when Brandy went berserk: sinking his teeth into the

neck of one horse, causing it to buck and dump its rider, the enraged stallion reared up and lashed out with its forelegs. The second horse, an amiable cow pony, stumbled and went down, struck in the head by one of the Morgan's hoofs; another flailing hoof broke the leg of its rider. He pitched from the saddle, collapsing in the water with a scream, only to die a moment later trampled under by the raging stallion.

Ashore, the other rustlers ran to grab their rifles. But they were too slow: Brandy had already scrambled up the opposite bank and was racing off across the valley, one of the riders' ropes trailing from his neck.

'Get after him!' someone yelled. Half a dozen rustlers sprang into their saddles and spurred their mounts after the stallion. But no ordinary horse or cow pony could catch the Morgan. Brandy reached the north end of the basin while his pursuers were still a hundred yards behind.

A wall of rock and brush loomed up before the stallion. For a moment he seemed trapped. Then picking up the scent of the mustangs, he followed it to the entrance of the narrow pass. Barely slowing down, he raced on through the pass and out the other end into the desert beyond.

For the first time in his life Brandy was free. Exhilarated, he tossed his head, gave a long shrill whinny and galloped off across the open wasteland . . . rope trailing in the dust.

CHAPTER FIFTEEN

Dawn was breaking. Rays from the rising sun, barely visible above the mountains, poked holes in the overcast sky, turning the edges of the dark clouds a shimmering gold.

There was now enough light for Raven and the old wrangler to see Stadtlander's mansion silhouetted atop the low hill above them. Riding double, they crested the hill and rode quietly between the corrals and outer buildings. Save for the hooting of an owl, which came from the roof of the bunkhouse, the place was silent.

The old wrangler reined his horse up behind the barn. Dismounting, he and Raven crept alongside the side wall and peered around the edge of the big wooden building. It faced west, away from the dawn light, and at first they couldn't see anyone. Then a match flared between cupped hands that lifted it to the end of a cigarette. Momentarily, the weathered face of the cowboy smoking was outlined by the flame; then, as he blew the match out and flicked it away, darkness returned.

But now their eyes were accustomed to the half-light and they could see the man's profile as he leaned back against the double doors. The old wrangler reached for his six-gun. Raven grabbed his wrist and shook her head, no. She then pulled out her slingshot, took a pebble from her pocket and loaded it into the pouch. Taking careful aim, she let loose.

The pebble struck the cowboy on the temple. He crumpled and collapsed on the ground without a sound.

The old wrangler looked impressed. 'Sister, remind me not to turn my back on you.' Grabbing the cowboy's boots, he waited for Raven to quietly open one of the big double doors and then dragged the unconscious man into the barn.

Raven ducked in after them. Remembering her vision, she quickly looked around for Gabriel and saw him tied to the post. His face was badly bruised and swollen and she almost gasped. Still groggy, he was shocked to see her. She raised her finger to her lips, silencing him. Then standing in front of Gabriel so he couldn't be seen, she pointed to the unconscious cowboy and asked the old wrangler if he wanted her to find a rope so they could tie him up.

The old wrangler nodded, closed the door and leaned over to take the cowboy's gun from its holster. Behind him, Raven grabbed a long-handled shovel and swung it with all her strength. The flat side of the blade struck the old wrangler across the back of the head, dropping him. He lay where he fell, face down on the straw-covered floor.

Raven dropped the shovel, ran to Gabriel's side and hugged him.

Excruciating pain knifed through his ribs, making him grunt. But just to have her safely with him was worth all the pain in the world and he made no attempt to push her away.

'Oh, Gabe, Gabe . . . I'm so glad to see you. Are you all right?'

He nodded, teeth gritted against the intense pain.

'I thought you were . . . I mean, I didn't know if . . . I was so worried about you and.'

'Untie me,' he said, wincing.

Quickly kneeling behind him, she untied him from the post. 'I got a horse outside. Think you can ride?'

'Sure.' He winced as she helped him up. 'How'd you know I was here?'

'I . . . uh—' Raven hesitated, reluctant to reveal she'd had a vision. 'Almighty Sky told me. He saw you in a peyote dream.'

'Seems like that ol' Indian's always comin' to my rescue.'

'Mine too. Here,' she added as he took a step, grimaced, and held his side, 'let me help you.'

'No, you get their guns.' Limping to the door, he opened it a crack and peered out. Lights showed in the mansion. Men could be heard stirring in the bunkhouse. Suddenly the door was flung open and two hands stepped out, laughing, playfully pushing each other around.

'Hurry,' Gabriel said. 'This place is about to become a gully-buster.'

She quickly handed him the pistols. Making sure they were loaded, he tucked one in his belt then he and Raven ducked outside.

CHAPTER SIXTEEN

The old wrangler's horse was still tied behind the barn. Raven helped Gabriel climb into the saddle and swung up behind him. Crouched low over the horse's back they rode slowly between the outer buildings and corrals. Neither spoke, hoping not to disturb the stock penned up in them. Luck seemed to be riding with them. They had cleared the cattle pens and were a short distance from the big arched entrance – when three Double SS night riders crested the hill and rode in.

All were yawning and only half-awake and it took them a moment to notice Gabriel and Raven reined up before them; in that moment Gabriel drew both pistols and leveled them at the night riders.

'We can do this easy or hard,' he said. 'So either jerk your guns or hold your hands where I can see 'em.'

As one, the three weary night riders raised their hands chest high.

Gabriel nudged his horse forward, eyes fixed on the riders, ready to shoot the first man who moved.

None of them did. Gabriel reined up behind them, half-turned in his saddle as he said: 'Now, ride on like nothin' happened. An' remember, I'll be watchin' you. So don't do nothin' foolish.'

He waited for them to ride on a short distance then faced front and was about to spur his horse out of the gate, when a fourth night rider came riding up the hill. He wasn't as sleepy as the other riders, and on seeing Gabriel he instantly went for his pistol.

Gabriel shot him. The rider pitched from the saddle, rolled over in the dirt and lay still.

Behind Gabriel, the three riders grabbed their guns and opened fire. His horse went down, kicking and squealing. Gabriel and Raven were thrown to the ground. Momentarily dazed, they crawled behind the dead horse and kept their heads low as bullets whined overhead.

Despite his sore ribs, Gabriel returned fire, dropping one of the riders and forcing the other two to jump from their saddles and dive under a corral fence. The gunfire brought the remaining hands busting out of the bunkhouse. Finding cover, they poured lead at Gabriel, pinning him down.

In the middle of the firefight, Stillman Stadtlander hobbled out of the front door of his mansion. Supported by crutches, he stood on the porch beside his foreman, John Welters, and ordered his men to stop firing.

'Gabe?' he yelled. 'Gabe, can you hear me?'

'I hear you.' Gabriel peered over the dead horse at his nemesis.

'John, here, says you got a young'un with you.'

'What about it?'

'Give yourself up an' I'll let her ride out of here, even give her a horse if she's afoot.'

'Forget it,' Raven said before Gabriel could reply. 'I'm not leaving so that ol' wolf can hang you.'

'This ain't about you,' Gabriel said. 'It's about me'n Stadtlander. Has been all along.'

'I don't care who it's about. You're the only person I got left in the world and I'm not losing you, no matter what you say.' Before he could stop her, she stood up and glared defiantly at Stadtlander. 'You want to shoot me, mister, go ahead. You already killed my father, might as well add me to your sins.'

Eyesight failing, Stadtlander peered across the open area separating him from Raven. Not recognizing her in the gray morning light, he said gruffly: 'You're not makin' sense, girl. I ain't shot a man in over ten years, and that'd make you too young to remember any killing I ever done.'

'I remember this one,' she said angrily. 'I was right there when it happened. You may not have fired the bullet,' she added, 'but I'm holdin' you responsible.'

Stadtlander looked at Gabriel, now standing beside Raven, his guns trained on the old rancher. 'What she's talkin' about, Gabe?'

'Your boy, Slade.'

'Slade's dead, damn you! No one knows that better than you.'

'This was a while back. Slade an' the Iversons got hog-killin' drunk in the Copper Palace an' shot up the town. Mr Bjorkman and his wife an' Raven, here, was on the boardwalk an' one of the bullets killed her dad.'

Stadtlander scowled, troubled by the memory. 'That's old news,' he blustered. 'You know well as I do, Gabe, the judge cleared Slade an' the Iversons of all charges. Said other folks was shootin' too—'

'He's a liar,' Raven broke in. 'They were the only ones shooting when my father was hit. I saw 'em. And they saw me. But they kept on shootin' anyway. As for the verdict, mister, everyone in Santa Rosa knows you put Judge Raleigh in office so 'course he's going to say your son's innocent. Even a lame-head like me knows that!'

There was an uneasy silence among Stadtlander's men. To a

man, they knew Raven was right and not one of them could look her in the eye.

Stadtlander shifted uncomfortably on his crutches. 'I'm mighty sorry about your pa, girl. And I'd do anything to bring his life back. But what's done is done. No one can change the past. What happened was just a fluke accident and it's got nothin' to do with what's goin' on here. Gabe gunned down my boy. He's got to pay for that an' I'll be black-damned if I'll let him dodge a rope this time.'

Raven's anger suddenly boiled over. Grabbing one of Gabriel's guns, she fired it – kept on firing it – at Stadtlander.

None of the bullets hit the crippled old rancher. But they came close enough to rattle him. Snatching his foreman's rifle, he went to shoot Raven.

Gabriel fired first, the bullet knocking the rifle out of Stadtlander's hands.

'Next one's between your eyes,' he warned.

It went deadly quiet.

Every ranch hand itched to pull his iron. But fear of Gabriel stopped them. No one moved. Sweat trickled down their backs under their shirts.

'Get two horses,' Gabriel told Raven. He waited for her to run to the corral then pulled a wad of bills from his money belt and tossed them on the ground. 'This'll more than pay for 'em,' he said to Stadtlander.

Enraged, the fiery-tempered rancher turned to his foreman. 'Shoot him! You heard me,' he raged when Welters didn't move. 'Shoot the no-good sonofabitch!'

'You shoot him, Mr Stadtlander.' Welters picked up his rifle but kept the muzzle pointed at the ground. 'I don't feel like dyin' today.'

'You gutless bastard!' Stadtlander spat in Welters' face; then turned to his men. 'A thousand dollars to the man who shoots him.' When there were no takers, he added: 'That's a thousand on top of the reward.'

Some of the ranch hands nervously licked their lips, tempted.

'Go ahead,' Gabriel told them. 'Your next of kin can most likely use the money.'

'I'll take your offer,' a voice said.

'Gabe!' Raven screamed from the corral. 'The barn!'

Gabriel whirled toward the barn and saw the old wrangler aiming a belly gun at him. Gabriel fired, even as he was still turning. The old wrangler staggered back, dead on his feet, his short-barreled pistol firing uselessly into the dirt.

A shot rang out.

A slug tore through Gabriel's sleeve.

He turned and saw Stadtlander clumsily trying to lever another shell into the chamber of his foreman's Winchester.

Gabriel fired, once.

The bullet punched a hole in Stadtlander's chest, slamming him back against the mansion wall. The rifle dropped from his arthritic, claw-like hands and he slowly sank to the porch floor.

He sat there, eyes wide with surprise, hands clasped over the hole in his chest, watching as Gabriel limped up to the porch steps.

'Damn you, Stillman,' he said grimly. 'Damn you to high hell.'

Stillman J. Stadtman didn't answer.

'Why'd you have to go an' press me like that?'

'He can't hear you,' John Welters said. 'Dammit, man, can't you see he's dead?'

Raven came running up and examined Gabriel's left arm. Blood seeped through his bullet-torn sleeve.

'You all right?'

Gabriel nodded, and looked Welters in the eye.

'Let the girl ride out an' then we can finish this.'

'It's already finished.' Welters turned to one of the men

gathered around him. 'Harland.'

'Yes, boss?'

'Go get Sheriff Forbes. Tell him Mr Stadtlander's dead.'

'Want me to say who shot him?'

'Harland,' John Welters said irritably, 'if'n I wanted you to say that I would've told you to say that. Now ride, blast you!' As the ranch hand ran off, the foreman told two other men to carry Stadtlander's body into the parlor. Then turning back to Gabriel, he said quietly and without fear: 'I never much believed in this quarrel. Way I figured it you already paid for that Morgan many times over.'

'Too bad your boss didn't see it that way.'

Welters gave him a hard look. 'Wrong was done on both sides, Gabe. So don't act like you're blameless.'

Gabriel knew he was right and absently toed the dirt with his boot. 'Won't argue that, John. But I don't intend to let the law decide my future for me.'

'Wasn't expectin' you to.' The foreman pointed at some horses milling around in the nearest corral. 'Cut out two to your liking. There's saddles in the barn. Then you'n the girl ride on out of here and don't never come back.'

'Got my word on it,' Gabriel said. With Raven beside him, he limped toward the corral.

CHAPTER SEVENTEEN

Brandy looked down from atop the limestone cliffs and surveyed the herd of mustangs in the ravine below him. The only vegetation was a few clumps of mesquite and a lone Palo Verde, the roots of which clung precariously to a dirt overhang along one edge. A chestnut mare was nibbling the bark off the twigs and two young pinto mares were grooming each other; the rest of the herd was gathered around a natural salt lick.

El Tigre was nowhere in sight.

Brandy, who had chewed himself free of the rope around his neck, now issued a challenging whinny. He wanted those mares. He was willing to fight for those mares. And he didn't care who knew it. Pawing restlessly at the dirt, he charged down the winding trail leading to the ravine.

The broomtails around the lick heard him coming. Raising their heads, they watched as the coal-black Morgan came barreling down from the ridge and without breaking stride galloped toward them.

All but the youngest had seen this happen before, a stallion, alone and anxious to prove his worth to the mares, appearing out of nowhere and trying to take control of the herd. The result had always been the same: after a fierce fight with their leader, the vanquished usurper limped off to lick his wounds and perhaps die. Nor was there reason to believe today would end differently; so after a curious look at the newcomer, the mustangs lowered their heads and resumed licking the salt from the ground.

Brandy was closing in on the herd when *El Tigre* charged out from behind some rocks. He came at an angle, cutting the Morgan off from the mustangs, and Brandy wheeled to meet him. Teeth bared, ears flattened, the angry leopard stallion hurled himself at his challenger.

Brandy met the herd leader head on. *El Tigre* was taller and rangier than the Morgan but not as solidly built or powerful. Both horses collided and both were staggered by the impact. But unlike previous challengers, Brandy wasn't knocked sprawling by the leopard stallion's charge – or intimidated. Quickly recovering his balance, he reared up, snorting, and lashed out at the raging white horse.

El Tigre responded, dodging the flailing hoofs and lunging in close to bite Brandy on the neck. The Morgan screamed, more from fury than pain and, twisting free, whirled and kicked the herd leader with his back legs. The white stallion went sprawling, the wind knocked out of him. Brandy rushed in to stomp him. But *El Tigre* had been fighting for survival all his life and before Brandy could take advantage of his fallen foe, the wild horse rolled aside, scrambled up and met the Morgan's charge head on.

Brandy, caught off guard, felt teeth rip his shoulder. He danced away, blood streaming down his gleaming black coat. *El Tigre* lunged at him again. And as Brandy tried to step aside the stallion rammed him with his shoulder, knocking the Morgan down. Instantly *El Tigre* reared up and stamped on Brandy, the hammer-like blows dazing him. He tried to get up but again the white mustang pounded him with his front hoofs.

Unused to this kind of fighting, Brandy desperately rolled on his back and kicked out with all four legs. *El Tigre* was driven back, giving the Morgan time to scramble up and ready himself for the next attack.

El Tigre reared up and lashed out at Brandy, expecting his challenger to shy away, intimidated. But Brandy avoided the flailing kicks, reared and kicked back. The herd leader reeled under the blows, recovered and then ripped open Brandy's flank with a vicious bite. Brandy retaliated, slashing open *El Tigre*'s withers.

Back and forth the battle raged. The ravine reverberated with their whinnying screams and the thudding blows delivered by their hoofs.

Like two fighters slugging it out, both horses refused to give quarter.

Gradually, the Morgan's weight and power began to wear the leopard stallion down. For the first time since taking over the herd, *El Tigre* found himself backing up. Encouraged, Brandy charged in and rammed the weary herd leader, knocking the white mustang sprawling.

He desperately tried to get up but Brandy was already on top of him, pounding him with his front hoofs. *El Tigre* rolled aside but Brandy kept after him. Again and again the enraged Morgan stamped on the leopard stallion until finally, dazed and beaten, white spotted coat spattered with blood, the exhausted herd leader stopped fighting.

Brandy kicked him a few more times and then backed up, teeth bared, daring the mustang to continue. *El Tigre* got to his feet but just stood there, defeated, legs trembling, chest heaving, head lowered, mouth slathered with foam.

Behind him the rest of the herd looked on in shock. For years their leader had been invincible. Now his reign was over. Their loyalty switched immediately. As one they trotted up to Brandy, the mares nuzzling him, the young males showing deference by keeping their heads lowered.

Brandy reared up, pawing at the air and whinnying shrilly, signaling to the herd that he was their new leader. He then bluffed a charge at *El Tigre*. The white stallion shied away and retreated, offering no resistance. Brandy charged him again, chasing the defeated mustang farther away. Then he triumphantly returned to the lick, clambered onto a flat rock and proudly stood guard over his herd.

El Tigre, now an outcast, turned and dejectedly limped off.

CHAPTER EIGHTEEN

It was shortly after noon when Gabriel and Raven rode into Valley Verde.

Reining up just inside the entrance that was guarded by towering red cliffs on both sides, they dismounted behind some boulders and found an opening through which they could observe the rustlers.

Favoring his bruised ribs, Gabriel handed his field glasses to Raven. She focused them on the rustlers. All but two of them sat beside the stream, smoking and passing a bottle around. The two stood talking to Lucius Eldon, a tall silver-haired horse rancher in an expensive fringed leather jacket, tan pants, hand-tooled boots and a cream-colored Stetson.

'That's them,' Raven said. 'And those are the same stolen horses. But I don't see Brandy anywhere. Here, you take a look.'

Gabriel trained the glasses on the herd and nodded in agreement.

'Where could he be? I know he was with them. I saw two men riding off with him.' She took back the glasses and focused them on Lucius Eldon. He and the two men were arguing over something. 'Wonder who that man is – the one with the silvery white hair, I mean. I've never seen him before.'

'Let me see.' Gabriel focused the glasses on Lucian Eldon in time to see him handing money to the two rustlers. 'Reckon he's the buyer.'

'You think he's already bought Brandy an' taken him away?'

Gabriel shrugged and returned the glasses to Raven. 'Wait here, scout.'

90

'Where you going?'

'Water my horse. Those jaspers don't know me an' maybe I can figure a way to find out what happened to Brandy. You want him back, don't you?' he said as she started to protest.

'More than anything.'

'Then do like I say.' Handing her his Winchester, he added: 'Keep watchin' me through the glasses. You see me scratch my ear, trigger a couple of rounds my way.'

'You want me to shoot at you?'

'Not at me. But close enough to show the rustlers you mean business. I'll handle it from there.' Mounting, he spurred his horse into the valley.

Raven rested the rifle against the rock and picked up the field glasses. Focusing them on Gabriel, she watched him growing smaller and smaller.

Keeping his horse at an easy lope, Gabriel rode toward the creek. The land was flat. Scattered clumps of sunburned grass and greasewood poked up through the sand. There was no cover except for a few rocks. Gabriel made sure the rustlers saw him coming and kept his hands away from his Colt.

As he drew near the creek he slowed his horse to a walk and casually gestured to the nearest rustlers. They acknowledged him with surly nods. At the same time the silver-haired buyer turned away as if he didn't want to be identified.

Gabriel rode into the middle of the shallow creek and reined up, allowing his horse to drink. Remaining in the saddle, he took out the makings and rolled himself a smoke. Out the corner of his eye he saw several of the rustlers, all carrying rifles, approaching on foot. Striking a match on the horn, Gabriel lit up, lazily crossed one leg over the saddle and grinned at them.

'Afternoon, gents,' he said amiably. 'Sure is a hot one, ain't it?'

The rustlers made no attempt to answer. They closed in menacingly, not a friendly face among them. Gabriel showed no sign of tension. But he realized he might have overplayed his hand and prepared to shoot as many of them as he could.

A tall, hatless, scrub-bearded rustler in an old sun-bleached duster separated himself from the others. He looked up at Gabriel with dark, unforgiving eyes. 'Where you headed, mister?'

'Santa Rosa.'

'You won't find it in this valley.'

'I know. But first I got to slap a rope on this stallion I'm after . . . a runaway. Been trackin' him for more than a week now an' he's still runnin' free as the wind.' He eyed the herd of stolen horses grazing beside the creek. 'Could use a fresh set of legs if the price is right. My horse has been run ragged.'

'They ain't for sale.'

Gabriel shrugged, flipped his butt into the creek and rested his hand casually on his thigh, inches from his Peacemaker.

'Don't suppose you or your men have seen my runaway,' he said quietly. 'A purebred, black as a raven's wing an' mean as spit.'

Though the tall rustler didn't answer right away Gabriel saw the other men swap uneasy glances and knew he'd struck pay dirt.

'What makes him your horse, mister?'

'Won him in a poker game. Aces an' eights.'

'Dead man's hand.'

'Only if your name's Hickock. Me, luckiest hand I ever had. Well,' Gabriel uncrossed his leg and slid his boot into the stirrup, 'better be ridin'. I caught a glimpse of that black bonehead this mornin', but since then—'

'Mister,' the tall wrangler said softly, 'you're a damned liar.'

Gabriel frowned, as if surprised by the slur, and scratched his ear.

'That's a word I take offense to.'

'Then I'll say it again. You're a damned—'

Two distant shots rang out. Bullets whined off the nearby rocks, causing Lucius Eldon and the rustlers to hit the ground. The tall rustler ducked behind Gabriel's horse and looked off toward the entrance.

He only looked away for an instant but when he turned back he found himself looking into Gabriel's .45. The tall rustler froze and then slowly, grudgingly raised his hands.

'It's one against twelve, mister.'

'Three,' corrected Gabriel. 'That rifle didn't fire by itself. An' then there's my Uncle Cass up there on the cliffs' – he indicated the mesa to his left – 'He can shoot a fly off your ear with that Sharps of his.'

The tall rustler looked uneasily about him. 'You're bluffin', mister. There ain't nobody—'

Gabriel scratched his ear again and instantly Raven fired another shot, the bullet kicking up dirt near the tall rustler's boots. He jumped, cursing, and before he could speak again Lucius Eldon came walking toward Gabriel.

He was a handsome, refined man with a neatly clipped mustache as silver as his wavy hair. 'Tell your men to stop shooting,' he said as if he were accustomed to giving orders.

Gabriel held one hand up, hoping Raven would understand his signal.

'What exactly is it you want?' Eldon demanded.

'My horse back.'

'Go ahead,' Eldon gestured at the herd. 'Cut it out. Then go on your way.'

'Be happy to, mister, but he ain't there.'

'Then why are you harassing us?'

'Ask him,' Gabriel nodded at the tall rustler.

'He's lookin' for that black stud I told you about,' the tall rustler explained, 'the purebred that stomped Owens an' then run off up there somewhere.' He thumbed toward the closed end of the basin.

'Is that true?' Eldon asked Gabriel. 'Does that fit the description of the animal you're looking for?'

'Pretty much.'

'Then you're out of luck. Zach is telling the truth. The black was gone when I arrived. By now he's probably ten miles from here.'

Gabriel looked at the impenetrable wall of rocks. 'My horse is nimble, mister, but he'd have to be part goat to climb over them cliffs.'

'He wouldn't have to climb over them, friend. There's a natural cut in the base there,' Eldon pointed to the brush and rocks hiding the pass. 'Mustangs have been using it for years. I know. I've spent many long days in the saddle trying to catch their leader, *El Tigre.*'

Sensing he was telling the truth Gabriel holstered his Colt. 'Reckon I'll be on my way then,' he said. Wheeling his horse around, he spurred it into a lope and rode back to Raven.

CHAPTER NINETEEN

Raven was thrilled to hear that Brandy had escaped the rustlers, but not so thrilled when Gabriel told her the Morgan was running loose in the desert beyond the north end of the basin, an area that covered hundreds of square miles with little water or vegetation, but plenty of marauding mountain lions.

Alarmed, she insisted they search for Brandy right away. And when Gabriel warned against rushing off half cocked without a plan, she lost her temper and called him mean and selfish and uncaring and said if he didn't want to help her, fine, then she'd go find the Morgan on her own.

'Calm down,' he said, trying to be patient. 'Caution's the way.'

'Caution's *not* the way!' she said angrily. 'While you're being cautious Brandy could be wandering around lost or dyin' of thirst or . . . or being eaten alive by a lion or a bear!'

'No bears around here, black or griz'. They're mostly in the woods an' the high country to the north.'

She was in no mood to quibble. Mounting, she demanded to know if he was coming with her or not. He shrugged, stepped into the saddle and told her to lead the way.

Raven kicked her horse into a gallop and rode on around the base of the towering horseshoe-shaped mesa. Gabriel followed at an easy gait and after a mile or so caught up with her laboring horse. Embarrassed, she refused to look at him. But she grudgingly slowed her horse to match the pace of Gabriel's mount and together they rode to the north end of the mesa. There, confronted by a seemingly unbroken wall of rock, they dismounted and searched for the pass through which Brandy had escaped. The lower slopes were steep and covered with scrub-brush and eons of fallen rocks.

They had a large area to search and climbing was difficult, especially for Gabriel who was nursing his sore ribs. But after an hour of scrambling up and down over loose shale that constantly caused them to lose footing, Raven finally found the pass.

Though both were exhausted and soaked with sweat, she immediately wanted to start looking for Brandy's tracks. But Gabriel insisted they get out of the broiling sun and rest for a spell. Despite her impatience, this time Raven didn't argue. They found some shade under a rocky overhang and sat there for a while, sipping warm, iron-tasting water from their canteens.

The wait drove Raven crazy. Restless as a fire ant, she kept fidgeting around, changing positions, grumbling to herself, until she realized Gabriel couldn't be hurried. Then she settled down and sat with her tanned arms clasped about her upraised knees, staring out across the arid, sun-scorched wasteland, trying to imagine which direction the Morgan had taken.

'If you were Brandy,' she asked Gabriel, 'which way would you go?'

Hat covering his eyes, hands folded behind his head, he was silent so long she thought he'd fallen asleep. Southeast, he said finally, adding but that was because he knew where the Rio Grande was and where the grass was sweetest. Brandy would know that too, wouldn't he, Raven said. When Gabriel shrugged, she pinned him down, saying that since he had ridden Brandy for years it only made sense that any place Gabriel went the Morgan went too. Which meant Brandy knew as much as he did.

Gabriel raised his hat and scowled at her. 'You sayin' that dumb horse is as smart as me?'

'I'm saying,' Raven said, 'that Brandy's smart, a lot smarter than you give him credit for, and he'd remember something as important as good grass and plenty of water.'

Either because he'd had enough of her yapping or because he felt they were rested, Gabriel suddenly got up, brushed the dirt from his backside and descended the slope to the horses. Caught off guard Raven chased after him, sliding, stumbling, and finally slithering on her backside down the loose shale to the bottom.

Scrambling to her feet, she brushed herself off and hurried after Gabriel. He didn't say anything but the look he gave her made her mad.

'I'm warning you, Gabe. You tell me "caution's the way" one more time and by all that's holy, I'll shoot you.'

The wasteland was baked hard by the relentless sun, and

constant winds kept much of it covered with a fine layer of sand, making it almost impossible to spot any hoofprints. But as a young outlaw hiding out in Mexico, Gabriel had learned tracking from the Raramuri, a tribe of reclusive Indians living in the Copper Canyon area of the Sierra Madre. Famous for pursuing their prey on foot until it collapsed from exhaustion, The Runners, as the Raramuri called themselves, were the finest trackers in the world.

Raven looked on in amazement as Gabriel, walking hunched over, carefully examined the ground. Scraping sand away here, spotting a bent blade of scorched grass there, finding a crumpled cactus spine or crushed yellow petal from a flowering Cholla, it didn't take him long to pick up Brandy's hoofprints. And when Raven wanted to know how he knew the prints belonged to Brandy and not some wandering broomtail, he pointed out two different hoofprints and explained that the Morgan's shoes left a more distinct imprint than those of an unshod mustang. Thoroughly impressed, she didn't argue when he told her to get mounted. He then stepped into the saddle himself and together they slowly rode alongside the trail of hoofprints, heading in the direction taken by Brandy.

CHAPTER TWENTY

They rode until darkness made tracking impossible. By then they had covered better than ten miles and still hadn't caught a glimpse of the Morgan. But just before dusk they did see buzzards circling above an all-white stallion limping across a dry riverbed about a quarter mile to their left. Surprised to see an injured mustang alone in this part of the desert, Gabriel focused his field glasses on it. Realizing its uniqueness, he quickly handed the glasses to Raven and explained what breed it was.

She'd never seen any kind of Appaloosa before, let alone a rare leopard stallion, and was fascinated by the speckling of pinkish-brown spots.

'Oh, no, it's hurt,' she said suddenly. 'No wonder the poor thing's limping. Here, take a look,' she gave him the glasses. 'It's covered in cuts an' there's blood running down its withers.'

Gabriel focused the glasses on the mustang and realized Raven was right. 'Most likely been in a fight.'

'Maybe Apaches tried to kill it for meat.'

'Uh-uh. Indian gets close enough to use his knife, next step is the cookin' pot. Nah,' he said after another look, 'this fella's been in a fracas. Over another stallion's mares, I'll bet. Got the worst of it, too, or he'd still be with the herd. Shame,' he added, eyeing the big ugly birds tirelessly circling aloft. 'Right fine lookin' horse.'

Raven made a decision. 'Give me your rifle, Gabe.'

'If you're thinkin' of putting it out of its misery, the buzzards and coyotes will do that.'

'I didn't leave *you* to the buzzards,' she reminded. 'Or the coyotes. And you ain't half as pretty as that horse. Now, give me your dang rifle.'

There was a stubborn set to her mouth and jaw and Gabriel knew he wasn't going to change her mind. 'You ever shot a horse, scout?'

'No. But like my Dad used to say: always a first time for everything.'

Admiring her courage at that moment, Gabriel returned the field glasses to his saddle-bag, and said: 'What do you say we do it together?'

*

El Tigre heard them coming. Weak from loss of blood, the mustang still managed to galvanize itself into action and galloped farther along the sandy riverbed. But his stamina was gone and after a hundred yards or so he came to a halt and stood there, flanks heaving, legs trembling, blood-flecked foam spraying from its nostrils.

Gabriel and Raven dismounted a short distance away. Telling Raven to stay put, Gabriel grabbed the rope hanging from his saddle horn, shook out a loop and slowly approached the all-white stallion.

'Whoaaa, boy,' he said softly as *El Tigre* shied away. 'I'm not goin' to hurt you. Whoa, whoa . . . easy now . . . easy. . . .' With a slow graceful flick of his hand, he tossed the loop over the mustang's head and pulled it tight.

Instantly, the weary horse reared up, whinnying angrily, and tried to pull free. Gabriel held the end of the rope behind him, under his thighs as if he were sitting on it, and dug his heels into the dirt. The stallion dragged him along the wash for a short distance. Then Gabriel's weight became too much for him and, exhausted, he stopped and stood there, snorting, pink eyes glaring at Gabriel, pawing at the dirt with his foreleg.

'Poor baby,' Raven said. 'He's all wore out.'

'Me too,' said Gabriel, sweat pouring off him. 'So forget the hearts an' flowers music an' tell me what you want to do with him.'

'What I want to do?'

'He's your horse.'

'M-My—? You mean that?'

'Up to me, he'd be coyote bait.'

The magnitude of owning a horse, a wild mustang as magnificent and rare as this one, momentarily staggered Raven and she was lost for words.

'We'll take him with us,' she said finally.

'Are you loco? Could be days, weeks before we find Brandy. This cayuse wouldn't make it. Not in his condition.'

'I meant to the cattle doctor in Santa Rosa. My folks and Dr Pritchard were friends. He used to come out to the farm and have dinner with us all the time. If I want, he'll fix him up and keep him for me.'

'I'm sure he would. But we're not goin' to Santa Rosa. We're trackin' Brandy, remember? Or ain't he important anymore?'

'That's a mean, hateful thing for you to say, Gabriel Moonlight. You know I love Brandy more than anything. It's just. . . .' Her eyes strayed to the leopard stallion, which, as if sensing his future was in their hands, was no longer fighting the rope. 'I hate to see him die when there's . . . no reason.'

Gabriel said nothing. But she could tell he wasn't happy.

Suddenly she dismounted and walked to his horse. 'You're right. Brandy should come first.'

'What're you doin'?' he said as she took his rifle from its scabbard.

'What's it look like – shooting him.' She looked at the buzzards still circling overhead. 'God may not give two hoots about how this horse dies, but I do. And he's not going to end up desert-kill, that's for dang sure.'

Gabriel sighed. 'Hold up,' he said as she pumped a shell into the chamber. 'Maybe you got a point.'

Raven, who'd been praying he'd stop her, lowered the Winchester and pretended to be vexed. 'You saying now you don't *want* me to shoot him?'

'I'm sayin',' Gabriel said, wearily clinging to the rope, 'that maybe we should consider our options.'

'Which are?'

'We could try to gentle him some – though gentlin' might cost you a finger or two.'

'Go on.'

'Give him water an' maybe wash his wounds, wrap that leg if he'll let us get close enough – which ain't likely – anything, just so he knows we're tryin' to help him. Maybe then we'll win him over . . . get him to trust us.'

'Then, what?' she asked impatiently.

'Find some high ground to bed down for the night—'

'High ground?'

'Storm's comin'.' He indicated the thunderheads forming over the distant mountains. 'Could be a lulu an' I reckon we don't want to find ourselves swimmin' all the way to Santa Rosa, now do we?'

'Santa Rosa?' she squeaked. 'M-Mean we're gonna. . . ? Oh Gabe, Gabe,' she exclaimed, hugging him. 'Thank you, thank you—'

'All right,' he grumbled, hiding the pleasure he felt from making her happy, 'cut it out. No need to act like Christmas came early or somethin'.'

'But it has, it has! Can't you see that? And he,' she said, meaning the leopard stallion, 'is the best present you could ever give me.'

Later that night, while lightning flashed in the night sky over the foothills outside Santa Rosa, Brandy stood on a ridge overlooking the Box M ranch. Though the big spread was several hundred yards off, the Morgan could smell the broodmares enclosed in the corral. Their musky scent aroused him and he nickered, quivering with anticipation. Except for the teeth marks on his chest and flanks, and the soreness in his neck and ribs from *El Tigre's* pounding hoofs, the all-black stallion was remarkably unscathed from the fight.

Again the wind brought the scent of the broodmares to his nostrils. He snorted and pawed the ground with his foreleg, his shoe causing sparks as it struck stone. He heard a whinny rising from the darkness behind and below him. Turning, he looked down into a narrow sheltered ravine where the herd was tucked in for the night.

Brandy watched the drowsy mustangs, knowing as he did that he was responsible for their safety, whether the danger came from man or mountain lion; but the smell of the broodmares was irresistible and, tossing his proud head, he started down the long slope that stretched all the way to the ranch.

The ground was soft and sandy, and the Morgan made little noise as he descended between the scattered scrub-bushes and clumps of Cholla. Reaching the bottom he paused, lifted his head and tested the wind. The air had grown damp and smelled of rain. The scent of man was also strong, as was the smell of tobacco and Brandy alertly pricked his ears and listened for any noises that might warn him of danger.

Nothing stirred.

Brandy cautiously trotted forward. Soon he was close to the outlying corrals and could see the white fences and the buildings rising darkly behind them. Since he was downwind, the broodmares couldn't smell him, but they heard him coming and stirred nervously. Jostling each other, they nickered softly and flicked their tails.

The night-watch, an old cowboy known as Smoky for the cigarette always slanting from his lips, heard the mares stirring and silently cursed them. Grudgingly, he rose from his chair on the bunkhouse porch, grabbed his rifle and the lamp from the hook above his head, and plodded toward the corral to investigate.

'Keee-rist,' he grumbled, 'why can't you ladies behave y'selves?'

Reaching the corral he peered between the bars, squinting to see what was agitating them. Seeing nothing threatening, he clucked his tongue and made soothing noises, trying to calm the mares. When that didn't work he talked softly to them, as if they could understand what he was saying, asking them if they could smell the storm coming or if they had gotten wind of a lion. As he spoke he rubbed the necks, flanks and muzzles of the mares that brushed against the fence, all the while reminiscing about the good old days when there were no fences and he and other young cowpokes drove herds of wild, woolly longhorns up from Texas all the way to Wichita, where at the railhead there were often so many steers the pens couldn't hold them all and the rest had to wait outside of town, turning the grassland into a sea of beef.

Finally, worn out from talking and satisfied the mares were safe, Smoky ambled back to the bunkhouse.

Halfway there he heard thudding hoofs and turned, just in time to see the all-black Morgan charging toward him. Old and stiff-jointed as he was, he dropped the lamp and his rifle and dived aside, rolling to safety under the fence of an empty corral. When he looked back, the lamp was out and the stallion had vanished like a nightmarish shadow into the darkness.

Heart pounding, Smoky crawled to the fence and peered between the bars. The lamp lay two feet away. As he was reaching for it, he heard the mares whinnying . . . followed by the sound of their departing hoofbeats.

Fumbling for a match, he lit the lamp and stood up, lamp held high so he could see the barn-corral. It was empty. Cursing, he ducked through the fence, collected his rifle and fired twice into the air. Then he ran to the corral, saw the gate was open and stared off into the darkness.

He could hear the mares galloping away, but couldn't see them. Then suddenly lightning lit up the sky and for a fleeting second he saw – thought he saw – a black shadow racing in and out of his vision. Then it was gone and he was left wondering if he'd imagined it.

Behind Smoky, men dressed in various stages poured out of the bunkhouse. Lights came on inside the ranch house.

'What in Sam Hill's all the shootin' about?' someone yelled.

'Smoky, you ol' fart,' another hand shouted, 'I'm gonna pound your ears if you fell asleep an' dropped your rifle again.'

Smoky turned and faced the angry ranch hands gathering about him. Some wore long johns, others just Levis, others were hopping as they pulled on their boots, and everyone yawning and rubbing sleep from their eyes.

Unperturbed, Smoky dug a half-smoked butt from his shirt pocket, stuck it between his lips, struck a match on his gold tooth and lit up – each movement slow and deliberate, like he was taking his time to make sure he had the full attention of his audience before speaking. Then, when the men were about to explode with impatience, Smoky spit out a stream of steel-blue smoke, and explained what happened.

Before he could finish their boss, One-Arm Charley Devlin, a Civil War veteran, stormed up and demanded to know what was going on. When no one answered him, but kept their eyes lowered and shuffled their feet, he grimly eyed the empty corral then stabbed his forefinger at Smoky.

'Goddammit, Forster, did you forget to close the gate?'

'No, Mr Devlin, sir,' Smoky said, 'I surely did not.'

'Then who the hell did?' Devlin glared at the other men. 'Somebody better speak up,' he warned when no one answered, ''cause nary a one of you is moving from this spot till I get an answer.'

'Shadow Horse,' piped up one of the hands.

'What?' said Devlin. 'What was that you just said, Harv?'

'Smoky, here,' another hand chimed in, 'says this wild, half-crazed black mustang come bustin' in an' damn near stomped him to death. Then, 'fore Smoky could stop him, it disappeared like a shadow—'

'Taking the mares along with 'im,' Smoky reminded. 'Don't forget that, boys. That's the most important part.'

Devlin erupted. 'A wild mustang opened the gate all by hisself an' let the mares out, is that what you 'pokes are asking me to believe?'

'Yes, sir, Mr Devlin,' Smoky said. 'I reckon it is.'

Devlin eyed him angrily. 'Smoky, it's a damned good thing you've worked for me a long time, 'cause right now loyalty's all that's saving you from pickin' up your wages. Get ready to ride,' he added to the hands. 'We're going after those mares.'

CHAPTER TWENTY-ONE

The storm hit shortly after midnight, bringing thunder, lightning and torrential rain that flooded the desert, turning gullies and dry washes into churning rivers.

Earlier that evening, Gabriel and Raven had made camp in a cave halfway up on a rocky hillside. Unsaddling their horses, Gabriel led them to the back of the cave where he fed them each a handful of grain. Raven tried to do the same with the leopard stallion. But though he'd quit fighting the rope and seemed calmer and stronger after drinking water from Gabriel's hat, he was still too wild to let them wash his wounds or feed him by hand. Finally, after he'd viciously lunged at her a few times, she left the grain on the ground in front of him and retreated. But that didn't win him over either. Ignoring the grain, *El Tigre* stamped the ground and aggressively flicked his flowing tail as if warning Raven not to come near him.

Watching them testing each other as he spread out the bedrolls, Gabriel couldn't help thinking how alike the two were.

Frustrated, Raven finally gave up and helped Gabriel cover their bedrolls with their slickers. The cave wasn't very deep and there was no way to cover the entrance. Both knew that once the wind really got to blowing it wouldn't be a matter of if they were going to get wet, but how badly. Meanwhile, her eyes never left the white mustang and when they'd finished and were sitting with their backs against the wall, eating jerky, Raven wondered aloud if the horse would ever trust her.

'That depends,' Gabriel said.

'On what?'

'How much effort you're willin' to make. Takes time to build trust. Time, patience, and respect.'

'Reckon that lets me out,' she said with surprising candor. 'Comes to patience, I'm worse than an armadillo diggin' for grubs.'

Gabriel chuckled and fondly ruffled her hair. 'Don't sell yourself short, scout. Set your mind to it an' you'd be surprised what you can do. Take us for instance. We banged heads early on. But once we learned to respect one another . . . to understand each other's ways . . . everything turned out fine. Wouldn't you agree?'

Raven nodded.

'Remember, anything worth having is worth waitin' for.'

'Caution's the way, huh?'

'No one's said it better.'

Raven didn't argue but she wasn't convinced. She chewed her jerky in silence, the beef so tough and stringy she almost gagged. Spitting it out, she grabbed her slingshot and announced she was going to kill something for the pot. Gabriel didn't try to stop her. He didn't have to. No sooner had she stepped outside when lightning lit up the sky, followed by rumbling thunder.

Though the eye of the storm hadn't reached them yet, Raven jumped back into the cave and plopped down on her bedroll. 'Just 'cause I don't like lightning,' she said as Gabriel grinned, 'don't mean I'm scared of it.'

'I'm scared of it. Don't mind admittin' it, either.'

'Phooee. You're just sayin' that to make me feel better.'

'No,' he said quietly. 'I'm scared of it all right.' He lit the cigarette he'd been rolling and leaned back against the cave to enjoy it. 'Once when I was a young'un in Colorado, Pa and me were ridin' up a mountain to one of the gold camps when we got caught in a thunderstorm. The mule I was ridin' got skittish an' bucked me off. As I was cussin' it, a bolt of lightning come down an' hit the mule 'tween the eyes an' killed it.' Gabriel paused, spit out a smoke ring and poked his finger through it. 'Been scared of Mr Lightning ever since.'

Raven giggled. 'Know what, Mr Moonlight? You are the world's biggest liar, bar none. But I love you anyway.' Leaning her dark head on his shoulder, she yawned and was asleep before he finished his cigarette.

Though he never would have admitted it, having her pressed against him warmed him better than any fire. Slowly, so he didn't wake her, he eased his arm up and put it around her shoulders. Let it thunder and rain all night, he thought. He didn't care. He knew Raven was the closest he would ever come to having a daughter. Just like he knew he'd never find another woman like her mother, Ingrid. But that was all right. Now he had Raven. And knowing she loved him, trusted him, respected him was like . . . well, like owning a little piece of heaven.

CHAPTER TWENTY-TWO

The next morning dawned clear and bright. Gabriel stood in the mouth of the cave and inhaled a great lungful of fresh, crisp, sweet air. The sky was already aflame with color, mauves, pinks, blues and yellows so vivid they would look unreal on a canvas, the distant mountains so sharply defined they seemed touchable, while the desert stretching flatly to the horizon had a sparkling scrubbed-clean look to it.

Scrubbed clean? The thought jolted Gabriel out of his revelry. He hurried down the slope and looked about him. The damp sandy soil was so smooth it could have been ironed. No tracks of any kind scarred the surface.

Christ on the cross, he thought. How could he hope to find Brandy when the rain had washed away all trace of the stallion's hoofprints?

The two of them rode in glum silence in the direction of Santa Rosa. Earlier, the leopard mustang had fought the rope when Gabriel tried to lead it behind his horse. But now, a mile or two from the cave, it seemed to have resigned itself to capture and gave him no more trouble. Gabriel didn't trust it however. From his experiences with the Morgan, he knew horses never forgot a slight and though they may act meekly, they were merely biding their time until they could seek revenge.

'Gabe . . . what's a cayuse?'

Her voice came out of nowhere, interrupting his thoughts so that he had to think a moment before answering. 'Indian pony, why?'

108

'Never heard the word.'

'Comes from the Cayuse Indians, a tribe in the north-west. Heard of that, haven't you?'

'Canada, you mean?'

'Close enough. A long time ago the Cayuse bred their ponies with huge French horses called Percherons. Their neighbors, the Nez Perce—'

'The who?'

'Nez Perce – means "pierced nose" – liked the spotted horses so much they started breedin' their own. Folks ended up callin' 'em Appaloosas, supposedly after the Palouse River near where they lived.'

Raven looked at Gabriel in awe. 'How come you know so much?'

'I don't,' he said. 'Reckon you could fit everythin' I know in a thimble and still have room for a gallon of coffee.'

'I'm serious. Where'd you learn so much?'

'Mostly from Pa. Used to read to me every night 'tween supper an' prayers. Said ignorance was a sin, an' it was his duty to keep me from burnin' in the fires of hell.'

Raven thought a moment before saying, 'He must've loved you very much.'

Gabriel gave a grunt that could have meant yes or no.

'I wish I'd met your pa,' she said wistfully. 'I bet I would have liked him. He sounds like my dad. Always wanting me to get smarter.'

'Brains is the way,' said Gabriel and he winked.

By mid-morning the adobe buildings of Santa Rosa could be seen peeking through the distant shimmering heat waves. Knowing they only had a mile to go, Raven reined up and begged Gabriel to find some shade and take a nap till she returned. By riding into town he was risking his neck for no reason. She didn't need his help to turn the leopard mustang over to Dr Pritchard, and if he rode in with her someone was bound to see him and tell Sheriff Forbes or one of his deputies, who'd arrest him.

Gabriel disagreed. The last time he was in Santa Rosa, he said, the sheriff and his deputies went into hiding until he left.

'That was a long time ago,' Raven reminded. 'Now there's two thousand dollars on your head. An' even if the law don't want to collect it, there are plenty of others who do, including bounty hunters. Rats like them are willing to hide in an alley somewhere an' pick you off as you ride by.'

Gabriel knew she was right, but he stubbornly refused to listen. First off, he explained, the reward was no longer two thousand. That extra thousand was Stadtlander's money and now he was dead. Raven didn't care. A thousand dollars was more than most folks in Santa Rosa made in a year. On top of that, she argued, there was border trash that would kill for a dollar, much less a thousand. When he didn't answer, she added, 'What happened to "caution's the way"? Or don't you listen to your own advice?'

He had no comeback. Before the argument could continue, they saw a group of riders approaching from town. Gabriel shaded his eyes with his old campaign hat and tried to make out who they were. When that didn't work he took out his field glasses and focused them on the party. He recognized their leader right away.

'Posse?' Raven asked.

'Nope. A horse-rancher I used to know.' Returning the glasses to his saddle-bag, he gave her the rope holding the leopard mustang and rode ahead to meet the riders.

One-Arm Charley Devlin, on recognizing Gabriel, signaled for his men to halt, warned them to keep their hands away from their guns, and then rode forward to greet him. ''Morning, Gabe,' he said cordially. 'Been a spell.'

110

'An' then some.' Gabriel shook the tough, stocky, ex-Union cavalry officer's one good hand. 'How's life treatin' you, Mr Devlin?'

'No complaints. Well, maybe just one. Last night a wild mustang raided my ranch an' stole a bunch broodmares—' He broke off, shocked, as he saw Raven riding up with the leopard stallion in tow. 'Jesus in a hand-basket,' he exclaimed. '*El Tigre*! If that ain't a sight for sore eyes!'

'You know this horse, Mr Devlin?'

'Damn right I do. Me an' just about every other rancher in these parts. How'd you throw a rope on him, little lady?'

'I didn't,' Raven said. 'Gabe did. Is that his name, sir, *El Tigre*?'

'That's what some call him,' Devlin said. 'Though *El Diablo* would suit him better. Mind if I take a closer look?' he asked Gabriel.

'Help yourself.' Gabriel half-turned in the saddle, his right hand never straying far from his Colt, and watched as Devlin rode alongside the white mustang. Instantly, *El Tigre* flattened his ears, bared his teeth and tried to cow-kick Devlin's horse.

Devlin danced his mount backward out of range, and sat there shaking his head as if he still couldn't believe his eyes. 'Know how long I've been after this fella?' he said to Gabriel. 'Must be two years, maybe longer.'

'He's not the one who stole your mares,' Raven said. 'He was with us all night through the storm.'

'Wouldn't matter even if he wasn't, little lady. Stallion I'm looking for is all black. And powerful mean.'

Gabriel and Raven swapped uneasy glances.

'You got a good look at him then?'

'My night-watch, Smoky Forster, did. Came close to being stomped by him. Said the horse actually tried to run him down. Damnedest thing he ever saw. Stallion then somehow got the corral gate open and ran off with my mares. Whole thing only took a few seconds. Then he was gone like a shadow.'

Gabriel again exchanged looks with Raven.

'Any idea where he is now, Mr Devlin?'

'Not after the storm hit, no. Rain washed the desert clean. But we'll find him, believe me. Tall Tree, here' – he thumbed at a sturdy young Mescalero in a white breech-clout, an old navy-blue flannel Army shirt and a red turban who was riding a paint – 'he can track a snake over rocks.'

Gabriel, who'd heard of Tall Tree, didn't doubt it. 'What happens after you find him?'

'I'll make sure that black devil don't steal any more mares, not from me or anyone else. Ever.'

There was an uneasy silence.

'Your night-watch,' Gabriel said finally, 'was he sure the horse was a broomtail or could it have been a purebred?'

Devlin, who'd seen the looks passing between Gabriel and Raven, wheeled around and reined up beside them. 'A purebred, you say?'

'A Morgan,' said Raven. 'Black as my hair an' not a speck of white on him.'

Devlin looked from Raven to Gabriel, saw how uneasy they were and said, 'All right, you two. What's going on? Tell me straight. Do you know something I don't?'

'Rustlers,' Gabriel said. 'They stole my horse, a purebred Morgan, an' somehow it got away from 'em. We been trackin' him since early yesterday.'

'And you think he's the one who ran off my mares?'

'Just a hunch.'

'Based on what?'

'How we found him,' Gabriel indicated *El Tigre*. 'He was wanderin' around in the desert, all cut up like he was in a fight, an' it's possible that—'

'The horse he fought was Brandy,' put in Raven.

Devlin snorted. 'That ain't likely, little lady. Horse raised in a barn hasn't been born yet could whip a wild mustang, especially one the likes of *El Tigre*. He's maimed or killed half a dozen rivals. Seen their carcasses myself, rottin' in the sun after the buzzards got their fill.'

'Not sayin' it is Brandy,' Gabriel said. 'Just that it could be.'

'What's your point?' Devlin said, frowning.

'I'd like to ride along with you. Make sure it ain't my horse 'fore you get around to shootin' him.'

'I'll go with you,' Raven said.

'Not this time, scout. I mean it,' Gabriel said firmly when she began to protest. 'You got your job. Get your horse to Doc Pritchard. Have him take care of those wounds before they get infected.'

'Then, what? Sit around waitin' for you to get back?'

Gabriel answered by handing her money from his money belt. 'Here, take this. Get a room at the Carlisle Hotel. I'll be back 'fore you know it.'

Raven took the money but didn't say anything.

Devlin stood up in his stirrups and signaled to one of his hands. 'Go with her, Jensen. Make sure she's taken care of.'

'I don't need nobody to take care of me,' Raven said angrily. 'I grew up around here for God's sake!' She spurred her horse toward town, *El Tigre* grudgingly loping along behind her.

Gabriel grinned ruefully at Devlin. 'She has a sweet side, too.'

Devlin chuckled. 'So did her pa. But the rest of him was pure down-home stubborn. How's *Mrs* Bjorkman?' he added as he and Gabriel rode back to the riders. 'Pulled up stakes and moved to California, I heard.'

Gabriel nodded. 'We lost her to typhoid,' he said grimly. 'That's why I'm ridin' herd on Raven.'

CHAPTER
TWENTY-THREE

Dr Ezra Pritchard's office was on the corner of Front and Oak Streets. Behind his office was a stable in which he examined and housed his four-legged patients, and next door, facing Lee's Food and Grain Store, was a rooming house run by Carlotta, his Mexican-born wife of forty-one years.

Doctor P, as his friends called him, was a small, mild-mannered, congenial man in his sixty-third year, with merry blue eyes, a bulbous nose kept red by constant tippling, and wisps of straggly brown hair that grew around his bald dome like a horseshoe. As Santa Rosa's only veterinarian, he was busy day and night, especially during spring foaling and, but for an addiction to poker, he would have been a rich man.

Now, as he examined a leggy, sleek sorrel gelding that had a stone bruise on its sole, he happened to glance up, and under the belly of the horse saw Raven standing in the open doorway. Taking a second look to make sure it was really her, he turned the sorrel over to his helper, a gimpy former buffalo soldier named Jesse Philo, and hurried out to greet her.

He was full of cheerful questions until he learned Raven's mother had passed away; then, as if her loss made him aware of his own mortality, he lost his exuberance, excused himself long enough to take a nip from his pocket flask, then returned and asked Raven what she wanted. She led him outside where the leopard stallion was tied up beside her horse.

Dr Pritchard's bushy eyebrows arched with surprise. 'My goodness, an Appaloosa! How on earth did you come by him?'

114

Raven quickly explained everything. Dr Pritchard listened without interrupting her, nodding occasionally, grunting 'uh-huh, uh-huh,' eyes fixed on *El Tigre*, until Raven concluded by asking if she could leave the injured stallion with him until it was healed and Gabriel returned.

'Of course, my dear. It's the least I can do, considering the number of fine meals your dear departed mother cooked for me over the years.'

As he spoke, Raven noticed a small, curious crowd gathering around the leopard mustang. Their chattering agitated *El Tigre*. He fought the rope, twisting his head and rearing up as high as the rope would let him, kicking and whinnying, until Raven lost her temper and shouted at them to go away.

'Never mind them,' Dr Pritchard told her. 'Let's bring him inside. Hopefully, he'll calm down enough to let me examine him.'

Untying the mustang from the hitch-rack, Raven spoke soothingly to him. He made no attempt to bite or kick her. But his pink eyes remained wild and fierce, and, ready to dodge any lunge he made at her, she gently led him into the stable. There, roping him to a post, she explained to Dr Pritchard that while she was waiting for Gabriel she was staying at the Carlisle Hotel. If he needed her for anything, he could reach her there.

Thanking her, Dr Pritchard had only one question: 'This Gabriel you refer to, who is he? I don't think I've made his acquaintance.'

'He's a friend of my mother's. They were going to get married, but then she got sick and ... an' ... now he's my guardian.' Beating the doctor to his next question, she added: 'Gabe's gone with Mr Devlin to hunt down a stallion that stole some of his mares.'

'Yes, yes, Shadow Horse, I heard,' Dr Pritchard said. 'Mr Devlin was here earlier, telling everyone what happened. Of course, it's not really that unusual, you know – wild stallions running off mares, I mean. Why, when I first came here in '77, ranchers were always complaining about—' He stopped as someone entered and came up to them.

He was a small, slim, handsome man who moved like a cougar on the prowl. Despite the heat he wore a black silk vest over his white shirt, string tie, gray corduroy pants and a black Plains hat set squarely on his head. He had two ivory-handled Colt .44s in low-slung, tied-down holsters and carried a new, expensive repeating rifle.

Raven recognized him immediately. And by his warm charming smile, she knew he recognized her.

'Why, Miss Bjorkman.' He doffed his hat revealing curly hair the color of pale ale. 'What a fine surprise. Last time I saw you, you were—'

'In Old Calico, I know,' she replied. 'How are you, Mr Rawlins?'

'Fair to middlin', thank you.' Latigo Rawlins replaced his hat and glanced about him. 'Yourself?'

'I'm fine. Gabe's not here,' she said as Latigo continued to look around. 'He's off in the desert somewhere with Mr Devlin.'

'I see.' The small, neat gunman studied her as if trying to read her mind. He had beautiful eyes, too beautiful for a man, with long fair lashes, but they were hard as marbles and the color of amber. They darted about, forever restless, and few could look into them without feeling threatened. 'Any idea when he might be back?'

'None,' Raven said. 'Like I was tellin' Dr Pritchard, here, he may be gone for days. Weeks even. But if you want, I'll give him a message when I next see him.'

Latigo chuckled, as if amused by her suggestion. 'Thank you, no,' he said politely. 'I always deliver my messages personally.' He turned to Dr Pritchard, adding: 'Did you figure out why my sorrel went lame?'

'I did indeed, sir. He has a mild stone bruise on his left front sole. I recommend you leave the animal with me for a few days. I can't guarantee I can cure him but I can definitely relieve some of the tenderness.'

Latigo nodded, satisfied. Politely tipping his hat to Raven, he left. He walked, she thought, like a coiled spring ready to uncoil at any second.

Dr Pritchard sighed as if an evil presence had departed.

'Is that man a friend of yours by any chance, my dear?'

'Uh-uh. He's a gunman, you know.'

'Yes, I guessed as much.'

'Gabe says he's the fastest he's ever seen.'

'Wouldn't doubt it . . . wouldn't doubt it for a second.' Dr Pritchard shuddered. 'He makes me feel like someone's walking on my grave.'

CHAPTER TWENTY-FOUR

For three days now they had searched every canyon, valley, water hole and plateau within a fifty-mile radius of Devlin's ranch for Brandy and the stolen mares, and found no trace of them. Worse, Tall Tree's superstitious nature had surfaced. The famed Mescalero tracker had overheard the riders talking about 'Shadow Horse,' and now believed they were trailing a shape-shifter. For all they knew, he might have turned himself into a mountain lion or an eagle and was mocking them from on high.

'Bad medicine,' he told Devlin and Gabriel as they camped in a ravine that night. 'Not know what animal we look for. Search forever. Never find.'

'Nonsense,' said Devlin. 'We're not dealin' with a shape-shifter or a shadow. He's a goddamn horse, like any other goddamn horse, and he's out there somewhere with my mares an' we'll find him.'

'Not true,' Tall Tree said solemnly. 'All die in desert if continue.'

'What makes you think that?' Gabriel inquired.

'Evil bird leave sign on rock. Say if we look more we all die from poison water.'

'Good Christ,' raged Devlin. 'First shape-shifters an' now evil birds. By God, I've had my fill of this!' He stabbed his stubby finger in Tall Tree's impassive face. 'Listen, you ignorant heathen. You signed on to find my mares an' you better find 'em or so help me Jesus I'll leather you with my chaps!'

'Easy,' Gabriel said, pulling Devlin aside. 'Won't get anywhere by threatenin' him. He'll just disappear in the night.'

'Then talk to him, Gabe. Make the sumbitch understand that either he earns his money or when we get back to Santa Rosa I'll have him thrown in the brig.' He stormed off to his bedroll.

Gabriel hunkered down beside the fire, rolled a smoke, lit it and handed the makings to the Mescalero. They smoked in silence for a while. The wind had died down and the night was eerily still. The only noise came from the occasional crackling of the fire, the snoring of a weary rider or a distant coyote yip-yipping at the moon.

Gradually, the flames flickered out. The glowing embers reflected redly on their faces. Gabriel waited patiently. It was strange, he thought. He had little or no patience when dealing with whites, but with Indians his patience seemed inexhaustible. Was there some significance to this?

Overhead, the moon hung like a luminous orb in an indigo sky. About them the rocky, barren hills shone like pewter. After an hour or so Gabriel rose, stretched the stiffness from his legs and then sat cross-legged next to the dying embers. He yawned, wondering as he did if the motionless Apache would ever speak.

Presently, Tall Tree began to rock back and forth. Gabriel ignored him. Next the young Indian took a tiny bag of yucca pollen from his pouch. Rubbing the pollen between his palms over the fire, he chanted under his breath in Apache. Gabriel couldn't hear what the Mescalero was singing but whatever it was it ended as abruptly as it started. Then as if protected by his ritual, Tall Tree stared off into the darkness and spoke to Gabriel in Apache.

'I have heard of you, Tall Man. Your name is known to The People.'

Gabriel, having learned from the Raramuri that it was rude to reply too quickly since the speaker may not have finished, kept silent.

'It is told around our fires that you were dying once and the Sacred One came to your side and begged *Yusan*, the creator of life, to return your spirit to you.'

'This is true,' Gabriel replied in Apache. 'Lolotea did save my life in this fashion.'

'It is also told that because of this your medicine is very powerful.'

'This also is true.'

'Almighty Sky has said as much.'

'This pleases me,' Gabriel said, 'for Almighty Sky is the wisest of all Mescaleros and would not say this if it were not true.'

Tall Tree nodded vigorously as if reassuring himself that he had nothing to fear. 'This medicine,' he said presently, 'would a man be unwise to believe it is powerful enough to protect him from the evil bird?'

'He would not be unwise at all,' Gabriel said. 'He would merely be proving to others that he has the courage to believe

119

what he knows is true.'

Again Tall Tree nodded, this time slowly and solemnly. 'It is as I thought,' he said after a long pause. Rising suddenly, he stepped over the ash-covered embers and melted into the darkness.

Dawn came. Like a silent, invisible brush it painted the dull gray sky with streaks of opalescent pinks and yellows that gradually turned the western slopes of the barren hills the same incredible colors. Even the faces of the weary riders, as they crawled out of their blankets, gulped a quick cup of coffee and saddled up, were tinted yellowy pink, so that everyone's skin had an unnatural glow.

'Well, you were right,' Devlin said as he and Gabriel saddled their horses. 'The injun didn't take kindly to my threat. Sumbitch has skipped.'

'I doubt that, Mr Devlin.'

'Then where the hell is he?'

'Lookin' for tracks most likely.'

'In the dark?'

'Full moon last night. More'n enough light for an Apache.'

'I thought Apaches were afraid of the dark. I was told they think if they die at night their spirits will get lost.'

'Just 'cause they're afraid of somethin',' Gabriel said, 'doesn't mean they won't do it; 'specially if they believe they're protected by powerful medicine.'

Tall Tree had not showed up by the time everyone was ready to ride. Disgruntled, Devlin decided not to wait any longer. With Gabriel riding beside him, he led the riders out of camp. There was only one trail out of the ravine. It led across a landscape as barren and pock-marked as the moon. There was no sign of life, not even the ever-present ants. All around them the desolate hills had been bleached white by the relentless sun.

They rode slowly, stopping every hundred yards or so to let Gabriel dismount and search the ground for hoof prints. But even his trained eye could find no sign of Brandy or Devlin's mares in the hard, ash-colored dirt. Finally, the trail dead-ended at the foot of a sprawling, rocky escarpment.

Cursing, Devlin called a halt. Everyone dismounted and drank from their canteens. They then wetted their bandanas and wiped away the salt caking their horses' muzzles. Devlin, knowing Gabriel knew the territory better than anyone save the Apaches, asked him if he thought they should go back or find a way around the cliffs. Before he could reply, Gabriel saw a familiar figure descending the rocky slope ahead of them. It was Tall Tree, rifle in one hand, a twisted piece of iron in the other, and Gabriel felt a sense of relief.

'Ask him,' he said, thumbing at the approaching tracker. 'Looks like he's found somethin'.'

'Dammit to hell,' said Devlin, exasperated. 'If I live to be a hundred and ten, I will never understand injuns. I mean, why the devil didn't he just tell us where he was going?'

'Trust,' Gabriel said. 'Apaches live by it an' expect us to do the same.' He waited for Tall Tree to join them. Their gazes met, each man silently conveying respect, and then the tracker held up his find.

It was a twisted horseshoe, with a nail hanging from it. 'Find on trail last night. Belong to saddle horse, not mustang. Fall off as run downhill. Recognize?' he said to Gabriel.

'Uh-uh. Ain't Brandy's.'

'Belongs to one of my mares,' Devlin said, pointing at the shoe. 'See, there's my Box M brand. Had my smithy make 'em special in case rustlers burned another brand over mine.'

'Smart,' Tall Tree said. 'Unless rustler eat horse.'

'Never mind the jokes,' Gabriel said, seeing Devlin was about to erupt. 'What about the mares? Did you find 'em?'

The tracker nodded. 'All horse other side of cliff. In canyon like box. They find water hole near rocks. No hurry to leave.'

'How big is the entrance to the canyon?' Devlin asked Tall Tree.

'Not so big. Wide as small river maybe.'

Devlin turned to his men. 'Boys, we'll block it off with rocks and trees an' whatever else we can find. That way, we won't have to worry about losing any of the mares when we round 'em up. Nice work,' he said to Tall Tree. 'I'll see you get a bonus.' He stepped into the saddle and motioned for his men to do the same.

The Apache looked questioningly at Gabriel. 'Not know bonus.'

'Extra money. More than what he promised you.'

'Why?' asked Tall Tree. 'I just find horse like he want.'

'It's his way of rewarding you. He knows how hard it was to track in this kind of terrain.'

The tracker absorbed Gabriel's words. Then, straight-faced, he said: 'Think I find mares too soon. Wait another day, maybe two, get bigger bonus.'

'Tall Tree,' Gabriel said, grinning. 'There's a lot of white man in you.'

CHAPTER TWENTY-FIVE

On entering the box canyon Gabriel and Tall Tree left Devlin and his men deciding where to build a barricade and quickly climbed to a ridge. From here they could see the herd gathered about the spring at the closed end. The water welled out from under some boulders, forming a shallow pool that minerals kept discolored.

Through his field glasses Gabriel identified Devlin's mares among the wild mustangs, but could not see Brandy. As if reading his mind, Tall Tree nudged the gunman's arm and pointed to a rocky ledge jutting out halfway up the cliff. Gabriel focused the glasses on it and felt his pulse quicken as he saw the Morgan standing there, proudly keeping watch over his herd.

'Go tell Mr Devlin that his mares are safe,' Gabriel told Tall Tree.

'You stay here?'

'For a spell, yeah.'

'Wise,' Tall Tree said, smirking. 'Hard work build wall in sun.'

'Get out of here!' Gabriel aimed a kick at the young Apache. But he dodged it and, laughing, hurried down the slope, nimbly jumping from rock to rock. Gabriel couldn't help chuckling. Once you understood how the Apache mind worked, you realized they had a wonderful, dry sense of humor.

Meanwhile, Devlin had divided his men into two groups: one lined up across the narrow entrance, ready to drive the horses back if they made any attempt to escape, while the others collected all the available dead wood and rocks with which to build the barricade. Devlin himself pitched in. He ordered Tall Tree to do the same, but the young Apache disdainfully refused. Trackers did not carry rocks. And after telling Devlin that his mares were safe, Tall Tree sat on a rock and smoked.

The men soon ran out of material on the floor of the canyon. Now they were forced to climb the steep slopes and pry larger rocks loose, so that they rolled down and piled up at the bottom. It was back-breaking work, made even harder by the broiling sun, and every hour Devlin switched the groups around to give each man a rest.

Shortly, Gabriel returned and joined the work force. As he

labored in the blazing sun he caught Tall Tree smirking at him. 'Keep grinnin' like that,' he warned the Apache, 'and I will make strong medicine so that an owl leaves you an evil sign.' Owls were the worst kind of bad luck and Tall Tree lost his smirk. Descending from the rock, he began working feverishly to win back Gabriel's approval.

By mid-morning the barricade was almost finished. Standing about six feet high, it had branches poking up along the top to discourage the horses from trying to leap over it. Finally, only a few more rocks were needed. Devlin impatiently yelled for the men on the west cliff to hurry. It was a mistake. A new hand named Tobler suddenly lost his footing and fell in the path of a boulder bouncing downhill. His scream brought the others scrambling to his side. He lay there writhing and groaning, his leg bent unnaturally under his body. His co-workers carried him down to the floor of the canyon. Here, Devlin had two men hold him still while he straightened out the leg. Tobler screamed in agony and fainted from the pain. Devlin bound the leg tightly between two straight branches and had him placed on a crudely constructed travois, which was tied behind his horse. He then told Tall Tree to take Tobler to Santa Rosa, adding, 'Tell Doc Carstairs to fix him up good an' charge everythin' to me. Understand?'

Tall Tree nodded and rode off with the injured Tobler.

Devlin then ordered the rest of his men to get mounted. Exhausted, they trudged grumbling to their horses.

'Men could use a rest,' Gabriel said.

The hard-headed rancher bristled. 'I don't pay men good wages to take rests, mister. I pay them to do as they're told.'

'Tobler did as he was told, Mr Devlin, an' got his leg busted.'

'Not my fault if some damn fool gets careless.'

'Responsibility starts at the top,' reminded Gabriel.

'Dammit, you telling me how to run my show now, gunfighter?'

'I'm tellin' you,' Gabriel said gently, 'that if some weary 'poke gets careless with his rope an' causes one of your mares to break its leg, you'll have to shoot it. That what you want?'

Devlin quietly seethed, but he couldn't deny Gabriel's logic. Striding over to his men, he grudgingly told them to take a short break. Grateful, they found what little shade existed, covered their faces with their hats and sacked out.

Devlin then rejoined Gabriel, who sat against a rock chewing on a piece of jerky, and began rolling a smoke. Finished, he offered the makings to Gabriel, who shook his head.

'You don't like me much, do you, Moonlight?'

'Ain't given it much thought, Mr Devlin. But I'd always heard you had a reputation for treatin' men fair and honest.'

'And you're taking it upon yourself to remind me, that it?'

'Caution's the way,' said Gabriel.

Devlin laughed disgustedly. 'Coming from a shootist with your reputation that's pretty ironic.'

'Just 'cause I spent most of my life makin' mistakes, Mr Devlin, don't mean I can't change my ways.'

Devlin had no comeback. He smoked in silence for a few moments. Then his impatience got the better of him. Rising, he stepped into the saddle, told his men to get mounted and pulled his rifle from its scabbard.

Gabriel immediately wheeled his horse in front of the burly rancher, blocking his path. 'You won't need that.'

'Don't push me,' Devlin warned angrily. 'You said your piece. Now get the hell out of my way.'

Gabriel didn't move. 'We're dealin' with broomtails, Mr Devlin – not Johnny Reb.'

'What we're dealing with,' Devlin said, bristling, 'is eight of my best broodmares. I paid a fortune for those horses and I'm not taking the chance of your stud goin' berserk and bitin' or maiming one of them.'

125

'Then let me go in first an' slap a loop on him,' Gabriel said. 'Once he's out of your hair you won't have any problem roundin' up your mares.'

Devlin glared at Gabriel, trying to rein in his temper. All around him his men nudged their mounts closer, hands on their guns, ready to back their boss.

'You really want it to come down to gunplay?' Gabriel said. Though he spoke softly there was a dangerous edge to his voice and Devlin, veteran soldier that he was, knew when to retreat.

'Easy, boys,' he told his men. Taking out his fob watch, he checked the time then said to Gabriel: 'Got thirty minutes. You ain't throwed a rope on that black devil by then we'll take him my way. You too, if you cause any trouble.'

CHAPTER TWENTY-SIX

From his rocky ledge, Brandy saw Gabriel riding up the canyon toward him. The Morgan reared, his shrill whinny alerting the herd of danger. Racing down the steep slope, he herded all the mares together and wheeled to face his former master.

Gabriel rode within a short distance of Brandy. Then reining up, he hooked his leg over saddle, rolled a smoke and flared a match to it. 'Don't know why I'm tryin' to save your life,' he said to the Morgan. 'Anyone with a speck of brains would just let Devlin shoot you an' save everybody a lot of fuss.'

Brandy pawed the iron-hard dirt and snorted defiantly at Gabriel. Behind the red-eyed black stallion, the herd milled around nervously.

Gabriel sighed. 'Reckon there's no easy way to do this, is there?'

Again the Morgan reared up, forelegs pawing at the air, and uttered a squeal of defiance.

'Figured not.' Gulping a last lungful of smoke, Gabriel exhaled slowly then flipped the butt away and unhooked his lariat from the saddle. 'Might as well get to it.'

He twirled the rope above his head and flicked a loop at the stallion. But Brandy was already rushing him and the rope spanked him on his withers and fell to the ground. Gabriel yanked on the reins, trying to avoid the Morgan's charge. The agile cowpony obediently crabbed sideways. But he wasn't quick enough. Brandy was already on him. Ramming him with his chest and shoulder, the Morgan knocked the lighter pony off its feet, spilling Gabriel from the saddle.

Gabriel landed hard. Winded, he looked up and through the swirling dust saw Brandy charging down on him. He rolled aside, barely avoiding the stallion's hoofs and sprang to his feet. Recoiling his rope, he swung onto his pony and waited for Brandy to charge again.

Brandy quickly obliged. This time the cowpony didn't need any urging from Gabriel. At the last instant he nimbly sidestepped the onrushing Morgan, and Gabriel neatly flicked his loop over Brandy's head. In the same motion he wrapped the rope around the saddle horn and pulled the pony back on its haunches.

The rope snapped taut, jerking Brandy off his feet. He landed on his back with a thud that echoed off the canyon walls. Squealing with rage, he scrambled up and prepared to charge again.

Before he could, Gabriel spurred his pony off at an angle, tightening the noose around Brandy's neck and pulling him off balance. The Morgan stumbled and fell to his knees. He struggled to get up but again was pulled over by the ever-tightening rope. Enraged, he rolled over and sprang up, at the same time throwing his weight against the rope. The lighter cowpony, even with Gabriel's added weight, was jerked off its feet.

Down it went, hurling Gabriel from the saddle. He hit the ground with stunning force. As he lay there, dazed, he heard pounding hoofbeats rushing toward him and knew it was the Morgan out to kill him. He rolled aside, avoiding the trampling hoofs, and scrambled behind a pile of rocks.

Half choked by the rope around his neck that was still attached to the saddle horn, the Morgan wheeled and rushed at Gabriel. Before he reached there he ran out of rope and was yanked back onto his haunches. His weight and momentum broke the cinch around the pony's girth and the saddle was ripped from its back. Glad to be out of the battle, the pony trotted off toward the barricade.

Gabriel ran around the rocks, keeping them between himself and the enraged stallion. Seeing the trailing saddle gave him an idea: scrambling over two boulders that were separated by a narrow space, he stood on the other side taunting the Morgan, goading it into charging him again.

Unable to pass between the rocks Brandy leaped over them to get at Gabriel. As he did, the trailing saddle became snagged in the narrow space. The rope went taut, jerking the Morgan backward in mid-air and slamming him to the ground. Momentarily winded, he scrambled to his feet and looked around for Gabriel. Seeing the man standing nearby, the stallion lunged for him but again was pulled up short by the rope. Trapped and half choked Brandy stood there, rope burns on his proudly arched neck, trying to regain his breath.

'Brains is the way,' Gabriel calmly told the panting horse. He sat on one of the rocks, took out the makings and rolled himself a smoke. 'Trouble is neither of us was gifted much in that department.'

He paused as he heard horses approaching. Turning, he saw

Devlin and his men riding toward him. Realizing he'd run out of time, Gabriel flipped his smoke away and went to meet the irascible horse-rancher.

Devlin reined up, his men behind him, and surveyed the scene. 'Reckon you got that rope on him,' he said to Gabriel. 'So I'll keep my end of the bargain.'

'Never figured otherwise.'

'One thing, though – I ever catch that black devil near my mares again, I'll shoot him. Understood?'

Gabriel nodded grimly.

'OK, boys,' Devlin gestured to his men. 'Cut out the mares an' drive 'em back to the barricade.'

'Why not take 'em all, boss, mustangs too?' suggested one of the riders. 'Once they're broken you can always sell 'em to the Army.'

'Good idea,' began Devlin.

'Not the mustangs,' Gabriel interrupted. 'They belong to Brandy.'

'Dammit, there you go again,' Devlin raged, 'tellin' me what to do.'

'Right is right, no matter who tells you,' Gabriel said. He made no move to draw his Colt but there was the same dangerous edge to his voice that had made Devlin back down earlier.

Not this time, though. This time Devlin made a stand.

'Mister, I've led men into battles I knew we couldn't win, an' I've spat in death's face more times than I got a right to. So knowin' you can put a hole in me faster than I can wink don't scare me one iota. Way I see it, I'm already living on borrowed time.' Without taking his eyes off Gabriel, he added to his men, 'Boys, wages I pay you don't include taking a bullet, so if any of you want out I'll hold no grudge.'

The riders stirred uneasily in their saddles, but no one rode away.

'I appreciate that, boys. Make your play,' Devlin told Gabriel. 'Otherwise, mount up and take that damn stallion of yours out of here.'

Behind Gabriel, the Morgan nickered softly.

Gabriel turned his head a fraction, enough to see Brandy watching him from nearby. All the rage had faded from his dark eyes, replaced by a curious look of trust – as if the stallion was expecting Gabriel to back him up.

Amazed by the Morgan's audacity, Gabriel faced front and prepared to draw, when someone called out his name.

Everyone turned and looked in the direction of the barricade. A slim, dark-haired young girl in jeans and a sun-faded denim shirt had just climbed over it and was now running toward them. As she ran she waved her arms and again called out Gabriel's name.

CHAPTER
TWENTY-SEVEN

Gabriel acknowledged Raven with a quick wave then turned back to Devlin. 'No gunplay while the girl's here. Agreed?'

'Goes without saying,' Devlin said. 'But find out what she wants an' then send her on her way, pronto.'

Gabriel waited for Raven to run up to him. 'What're you doin' here, scout? I told you to wait for me at the hotel.'

'I know. But I saw Tall Tree in town. Said you were here an' had found Brandy. So I rode out to see if he was all right.' Seeing the grim faces on the men around her, she added, 'What's wrong?'

'Nothin'.'

'Then why's everybody look so angry? Does it have anything to do with Brandy?' she asked when no one answered.

Gabriel put his hands on her shoulders and turned her toward the barricade. 'Go,' he said. 'That's an order,' he added when she didn't move. 'Get out of here!'

Raven angrily knocked his hands away. 'You got no right to boss me around!'

'Got every right. I'm your guardian. Now do like I say. Git.'

Ignoring his command, she stepped around him and approached the Morgan. 'What's wrong?' she asked, rubbing Brandy's muzzle. 'Why's everybody mad at everybody?'

The stallion snorted and jerked his head away, revealing the rope burns on his neck.

'Oh no, look at you,' Raven exclaimed. 'You're all raw and bleeding. How could you do that to him?' she said, addressing everyone. 'What's he ever done to you to be treated so cruel?'

'Little lady,' Devlin began.

'Shame on you,' she said, cutting him off. 'You're a horse-rancher, Mr Devlin. You're supposed to love horses.'

'I do,' he said lamely. 'But I got a right to protect my mares, from him or any other stallion tries to steal 'em.'

'But you got no right to shoot him,' Gabriel said. 'Or take away what's his.'

'You want those damn mustangs so bad,' one of the hands said, 'then buy 'em from Mr Devlin. He found them. He's got a right to do whatever he wants with 'em.'

'Forgettin' Tall Tree, ain't you?' Gabriel said. 'He's the one who found the mares, not your boss.'

'Is that what this ruckus is all about?' Raven said, 'a bunch of measly broomtails?'

'They ain't measly to him,' Gabriel said, indicating Brandy. 'He risked his life fightin' that leopard stallion for the right to run free with 'em.'

'Yeah, an' if I agree to let him loose,' Devlin said angrily, 'you know damn well what'll happen next: some night he'll be right back tryin' to steal my mares again. See my point?' he said to Raven. 'My back's against the wall.'

Raven thought a moment. 'I'll make a deal with you, Mr Devlin. You let Brandy an' them mustangs go free an' I'll give you *El Tigre*.'

'Raven—'

'Don't worry, Gabe, I know what I'm doing.' Turning back to Devlin she added: 'You said you'd been chasin' him for years now. That means you must want him pretty bad. Well, here's your chance.'

Devlin hesitated, obviously eager to own the leopard mustang, but. . . .

'Is it a deal or not?'

'I want the horse,' Devlin admitted. 'But I'm not sure I want him enough to run the risk of that black devil stealing my mares again.'

'That'll never happen, mister.'

'How can you be so sure, little lady?'

' 'Cause I'm taking Brandy an' the mustangs away from here.'

'And just how you planning on doin' that?'

Gabriel took a wild guess and said quietly: 'She's goin' to rent boxcars an' ship 'em out of here. Right?' he said to Raven.

'Right.'

'You know how much that'll cost you?' Devlin said to Raven.

'Don't matter,' she said loftily. 'See, what you don't understand, Mr Devlin, is I'm rich. Oh, sure,' she said when Devlin looked doubtfully at her attire, 'I don't look it. An' I sure don't talk like it. But my uncle back in Old Calico owned a bank and lots of land an' stuff. And when he was killed in an earthquake he left everything to Momma. And when she passed, she left it to me. Ain't that true?' she said to Gabriel.

'I was there when the lawyers had her sign the papers,' he said. 'She felt like it, she could buy a whole train.'

'Well, I'll be damned,' Devlin said. Dismounting, he offered Raven his hand. 'All right, little lady, you got yourself a deal.'

CHAPTER TWENTY-EIGHT

The morning sun was shining brightly when they pulled into Deming. The regular train was not due until after lunch and the windows and doorways of the station and the balconies of the adjoining Harvey House were crowded with curious people. They had heard rumors that a special train was coming and had seen its smoke curling up from far off across the wasteland.

Most of them were townspeople, white and Mexican, along with a few Apaches who had walked in from the reservation. They watched, fascinated, as Raven first unloaded her horse and then the all-black Morgan. Brandy, fired up by the excitement of the moment, was a little skittish but otherwise gave her no trouble and the onlookers applauded her skill. Next Gabriel and two hired wranglers unloaded their already-saddled horses; and then the gate of a second boxcar was opened and out poured the wild mustangs.

They came out in a panicked, wild-eyed rush, jostling each other as they clattered down the ramp, and were immediately herded together by the mounted wranglers.

133

Gabriel caught a glimpse of Sheriff Cobb and his shotgun-carrying deputy amongst the crowd, and threw him a half-salute. The sheriff tipped his hat to show he'd seen Gabriel and then pointed toward a saloon, miming that he would buy him a drink.

Gabriel nodded, and rode up alongside Raven. 'Any time you're ready, boss.'

Raven stood up in her stirrups and looked about her, first at the crowd, then at the flat, open land stretching in the direction of the Cooke's Range and finally at Gabriel. 'Let's go,' she said, ' 'fore I change my mind.'

Gripping Brandy's rope, she kicked up her horse and rode off toward the mountains. Gabriel signaled to the wranglers to move the mustangs out then galloped after Raven.

They rode at an easy gait across the wide plain for about three hours. The sandy gray soil was covered by a patchwork of yellow-green scrub-grass, clumps of prickly pear cacti, and tiny forests of yuccas. There was no cloud cover and the sun beat relentlessly down from the nude blue sky.

Stopping only to rest their horses and stretch their legs, they crossed the vast, open scrubland, cutting across gullies and dry lake beds ringed with lava deposits. Around noon they rested briefly in the shade of a scarecrow-shaped rocky outcrop. Here, they lunched on jerky and hardtack, washing everything down with tepid, copper-tasting water from their canteens.

At Gabriel's suggestion Raven kept a rope on Brandy, fearing the Morgan might make a run for it once they were in the open. But the stallion seemed to sense that what was happening was for his own good and made no attempt to act up. Nor did the mustangs cause any problems. They were content to stay with their leader, grazing on the dry, sunburned grass and green yucca shoots growing on the hillsides.

By mid-afternoon they entered a deep alkali draw full of tombstone-shaped boulders that was called the Devil's Cemetery.

They followed it for a mile or so, gnats flying about their heads, and then found themselves riding through an empty canyon flanked by cliffs of garish crimson rock.

Gabriel suggested they release Brandy and the mustangs here. But Raven insisted on pressing ahead. There was nothing wrong with the canyon, she explained. She just didn't feel it was the right place. When Gabriel asked her how she'd know what the right place was when she came to it, she shrugged and said: 'I don't know. I'll just know.'

The wranglers rolled their eyes, but said nothing.

They rode on.

Finally, after following a soft sandy trail along the base of a steep ridge, they came to a long narrow valley sheltered on both sides by craggy, red sandstone cliffs. There was an abundance of coarse green grass and greasewood, indicating the water table was high along with the possibility of a spring hidden among the rocks, and Raven instantly reined up and signaled for the others to stop. 'This is it!' she exclaimed.

Gabriel and the weary wranglers swapped looks of relief.

'Be sure now,' Gabriel said to Raven. 'Don't want to turn them broomtails loose an' have you go changin' your mind.'

'I'm positive.' She turned to the Morgan, adding: 'You like it here, don't you?'

Brandy snorted and tossed his head, his long black mane gleaming in the glaring sunlight.

'See?' Raven said. 'He agrees with me. From now on this is his home.'

Gabriel gestured to the wranglers, who nudged their mounts away from the herd of mustangs. The broomtails seemed to know they were free. They drifted apart, gradually forming a loose circle, and began eating the grass, tearing it up in tufts and swishing their tails to chase away the persistent flies.

Gabriel dismounted, sat on a rock and rolled a smoke. Raven

crooked her leg over her saddle, one hand still holding the rope around the Morgan's neck, and stared wistfully about her.

'We're doin' the right thing, aren't we?' she said after a long pause. 'Lettin' Brandy go, I mean?'

'It's what we agreed on,' Gabriel said.

'You don't sound too happy about it.'

'Don't have to be happy to do the right thing.'

'Ain't changed your mind, have you?'

'Nope.'

'It's the best thing for him, you know.'

'Yup.'

'Living with us in the city, whether it's San Francisco or Sacramento, would make poor Brandy miserable.'

'Ain't disputin' that.'

'Then what is it?'

Gabriel looked at the Morgan, met the black stallion's dark, solemn gaze and tried to explain to himself why he was sad about releasing a horse that always seemed intent on biting or maiming him in some way or other.

'I knew it,' Raven said, smiling. 'You love him just like I do. No, don't deny it,' she added as Gabriel protested. 'Can pretend all you want, call him all the bad names you like, hit him with that dirty ol' hat of yours an' even threaten to sell him for glue – it don't matter a hoot. You love him and he loves you, an' that's all there is to it. So, what do you think about that, Mr Gabriel Moonlight, sir?'

He exhaled a lungful of smoke and gave her a piercing look. 'My hat ain't dirty,' he said. Stubbing his cigarette out on the rock, he walked to his pony and mounted in one swift, gliding movement.

'Where you going?'

'Back to town.'

'Aren't you gonna say goodbye to him?'

'I already done that when I agreed to turn him loose.'

'Fine.' Raven watched him ride off, followed by the wranglers. 'Be an ol' grouch. See if I care.' Dismounting, she loosened the loop around Brandy's neck and flipped it over his head. 'You're free!'

The stallion shook his head, nickered, and pressed his muzzle against her shoulder. Then he was gone, like a loosed hawk, galloping off toward the mustangs.

Tears stung Raven's eyes. 'Dangit, pull yourself together,' she told herself.

A rider reined up behind her. She turned and saw it was Gabriel. She met and held his pale-blue gaze for a moment and then unashamedly broke into tears.

Gabriel dismounted and put his arm around her.

'I'm s-so mad,' she sobbed. 'I p-p-promised myself I wouldn't cry and . . . oh, hell,' she exclaimed. 'Hell, hell, hell. When am I'm goin' to grow up and quit being such a baby?'

'You done the right thing,' Gabriel said gently. 'An' I'm mighty proud of you for it.'

'It is the right thing, isn't it? I mean plenty of city folks keep horses, lots of horses, but you know sure as a bird on the wing they ain't happy.' She paused as Brandy now left the herd and came trotting up to them. 'Look,' she exclaimed, 'he's coming to say goodbye to you.'

Gabriel grunted, as if scoffing at the idea.

The Morgan stopped a few feet in front of them. He gently pawed the ground and nickered, at the same time lowering his head as if asking to be petted.

'Go on, Gabe,' she pushed him toward the stallion. 'Don't be so stubborn. Rub his nose.'

Suspicious, Gabriel hesitated.

'Go on, pet him. He wants you to.'

Again Gabriel hesitated; then, ignoring his instincts, he

137

reluctantly reached out to rub the Morgan's muzzle.

Instantly, Brandy charged him.

Gabriel tried to jump aside. But he was too slow and the Morgan playfully butted him in the chest, sending him sprawling.

Raven doubled over with laughter.

Covered in dirt, Gabriel sat up and angrily cursed the Morgan.

Brandy pranced around him, nickering as if amused, and finally stopped in front of the irate gunman. For a long moment man and horse stared at each other. Then the stallion tossed his head, whinnied, and trotted back to his herd.

'That's the funniest durn thing I've ever seen,' laughed Raven.

Rising, Gabriel slapped the dirt from his clothes with his hat. 'Lucky for him you were along,' he said, scowling after Brandy. 'Elsewise, I would have shot him.'

Raven only laughed harder. 'Should've seen yourself,' she said as he mounted his pony. 'Rolling over and over like a tumbleweed catched up in the wind.'

They rode to the mouth of the valley, where the wranglers awaited them, and looked back for a final look at the Morgan.

Brandy stood proudly posed on a flat rock part way up a hillside overlooking the mustangs. Maybe it was the fire in eyes or his wind-tossed mane, or maybe the way his coat glistened in the late afternoon sunlight like polished ebony, but for that moment he was everything God meant a horse to be.

Raven, overwhelmed by the sight, could only gape in silence.

Gabriel, noticing she was fighting tears, tried to think of something to cheer her up. But the way his quirky humor worked, all he could come up with was: 'Now I remember.

Wasn't buttermilk pancakes at all.'

'W-What?'

'I was wrong,' he said.

' 'Bout what?'

'Restin' on the seventh day.'

Tears forgotten, she gave him a puzzled look. 'What in blue blazes you talking about?'

'The Good Lord. Come Sunday He wasn't fixin' buttermilk pancakes, he was out in the corral creating Brandy!'

Raven laughed despite her mood. 'Without a doubt, Mr Moonlight, sir, you are the most long-windiest, sneak-in-the-back-door-thinking kind of person I ever met when it comes to explaining yourself.'

The wranglers chuckled and Gabriel smirked as if she'd complimented him.

Raven, more upbeat now, looked lovingly at Brandy. 'Think we'll ever come back to see him?'

'Reckon that depends.'

'On what?'

'If I can put up with your cantankerousness.' Winking at the wranglers, Gabriel nudged his horse in the direction of Deming.

'Hah!' Raven said, spurring her mount after him. 'You ask me, mister, it's the other way round.'

CHAPTER TWENTY-NINE

It was dusk when they got back to town. Paying off the wranglers, they took a room for the night at the Commercial Hotel. This time the pompous desk clerk made no discriminating slurs about Raven being a half-breed; in fact, he treated her with ingratiating respect, asking her if she wanted perfumed soap and bath water brought up to her room. Raven smiled graciously. That would be nice, she said. She nudged Gabriel, whispering that he could use a bath too.

Ignoring her, he accepted a Mexican cheroot from the desk clerk, flared a match on one of the lobby's cowhide lampshades and went across the street for a drink at *Los Gatos*. The little adobe cantina was crowded and noisy and Gabriel had to elbow his way up to the bar.

The barkeep greeted him cheerfully. But when Gabriel went to pay for his whiskey and beer chaser, the chubby mustachioed Mexican shook his balding head. 'Your money no good, *señor*. Sheriff Cobb say he pay.'

'That's mighty charitable of him,' Gabriel said. He gulped down his whiskey and prepared to drink his beer, when out the corner of his eye, between all the men lined along the bar he saw a familiar, unwelcome figure enter.

He didn't know why, but the sight of Latigo Rawlins disturbed him. He wasn't afraid of the handsome little gunfighter – he feared no man – but he did feel as if an icy hand had just gripped his jugular.

Meanwhile Latigo, who'd paused by the bat-wing doors long enough for his eyes to grow accustomed to the dimly lit cantina, now squeezed his way up to Gabriel.

'Heard you were in town,' he said amiably.

'From who?'

'Sheriff Cobb. I ran into him an' that nephew deputy of his outside the Baker Hotel. Said you and the young gal you run with had ridden off to set some broomtails free.'

'I don't "run" with her. I look after her.'

'Sure, sure, it's all legal. I understand. No offense meant.' Latigo signaled for a drink. While he waited for it, he rubbed a speck of dirt from his sleeve. 'I hear she inherited a heap of money.'

'Why would that interest you?'

'Everything concernin' you interests me, *amigo*.'

'Funny. Nothin' about you interests me.'

'You tryin' to rile me, Gabe?'

'Was about to ask you the same thing, "*amigo*".'

Latigo smiled, his teeth animal-white against his tanned skin, but under his long blond lashes his amber eyes grew hard as marbles. Waiting until the barkeep had set a bottle of rye and a glass before him, he carefully blew into the shot glass and wiped the inside clean with the tip of his yellow bandana. Then he poured himself a drink and raised the glass in toast.

'To soft saddles an' softer women,' he said. He downed the rye, held the empty glass up to his eye and studied Gabriel through it. 'I got to thinkin' the other day. You an' me, amigo, we're all that's left. Everyone else like us has been gunned down or, like Earp, rode west to California. We're dinosaurs, just like Sheriff Cobb says—'

'Rawlins,' Gabriel said bluntly, 'either button it or tell me what the hell you want.'

'To bend an elbow with an ol' pal, what else?'

'Bull!'

The word exploded from Gabriel and men all around them jumped back from the bar in alarm, fearing gunplay would follow.

'You'n me, bounty hunter, we were never pals.'

'No,' Latigo said softly, 'now you mention it, reckon we weren't.'

'So why you crowdin' me?'

Latigo turned and faced Gabriel, hands dangling near his ivory-handled six-guns.

'Fella has to earn a livin', *amigo*.'

The icy hand on Gabriel's jugular gripped tighter.

'The reward,' he said disgustedly. 'I should've guessed.'

'A thousand dollars is a thousand dollars.'

The cantina went quiet. Customers ducked fearfully behind tables and chairs. All eyes were riveted on the two gunmen.

'*Por favor, señors,*' began the fat-faced barkeep.

'Shut up!' Latigo snapped.

'*Sí*, señor. I shut my face.' Fearful, the barkeep crawled out from behind the bar and ran to the door, only to find his exit blocked by Sheriff Cobb and his shotgun-toting deputy.

'Appears I got here just in time, gents.'

'Stay out of this,' Latigo told him. 'Gabe an' me, we're about to settle some old business.'

'Not here. Not now,' Sheriff Cobb said. He stepped aside and two more deputies also carrying scatterguns entered.

'I got a legal right to collect the governor's reward,' Latigo said angrily. 'An' I intend to do it.'

' 'Mean you'll try,' Gabriel corrected.

'Move aside, Mr Moonlight,' Sheriff Cobb warned. 'I don't want you getting shot full of holes when this rooster tries to slap leather.' As if on a hidden signal, the deputies cocked their shotguns. The metallic click-click of their hammers sounded thunderous in the silent cantina.

Latigo Rawlins knew when to fold. Reluctantly lifting his hands from his guns, he tucked his thumbs in his gunbelt and kept his eyes fixed on Gabriel as he backed toward the door.

'I can wait, Sheriff,' he said mockingly. 'You can't protect him once he leaves Deming.'

'Protect me from what?' Gabriel said. 'You want to eat my lead, Rawlins, I'll be happy to oblige you.'

'Wait, wait, wait,' Sheriff Cobb said hurriedly. 'If you boys are so anxious to face off, then by God let's make a show of it.'

'Meanin'?'

'Play it like all the dudes back East think it takes place – a showdown. Main Street. Noon. I'll see it's fair an' legal. Hell,' he said as an idea struck him, 'I'll even get Pete Weyborne to bring along his shutter-box so he can record everything for history.'

Gabriel grinned mirthlessly. 'Still promotin' your memoirs, huh?'

'Why not?' Sheriff Cobb said shamelessly. 'The Earps and Clantons put Tombstone on the map. You two could do the same for Deming. It's no skin off your nose an' it'll make my rockin'-chair days more comfortable.'

'And at the same time do every lawman in New Mexico a service,' Latigo said, 'that the way you see it?'

'Won't deny that crossed my mind,' Sheriff Cobb said. 'But like I've told you boys all along. Your day's played out. Territory's growing up. It's got no use for mavericks like you anymore. By staying alive all you're doin' is standing in the way of progress.'

Latigo grinned at Gabriel. 'Has a way with words, our sheriff, don't he?'

'Yeah,' Gabriel said grimly. 'Way he paints it, us shootin' one another is pure downright noble.'

'Inevitable, not noble,' Sheriff Cobb said. 'Let's face it. Neither of you will grow old. Or die in bed. Only a matter of time 'fore some punk hoping to be another Charley Ford shoots you in the back. You know that well as I do. Only choice you got is how and where it happens.'

There was a long pause. No one in the cantina moved.

'Well?' Sheriff Cobb said finally. 'What's it going to be, gents?'

Latigo Rawlins cocked a questioning eyebrow at Gabriel, who shrugged.

'Noon's fine,' he said matter-of-factly.

'Gabe, no!'

Everyone turned as Raven, in her yellow gingham church-dress and matching hat and shoes, pushed through the batwing

143

doors and ran up to Gabriel.

'You can't! You promised Momma you'd take care of me.'

'An' I aim to,' Gabriel said.

'How? By shootin' it out with him? Maybe getting killed?'

Gabriel turned to the sheriff. 'Get her out of here, Cobb. Have one of your deputies take her back to the hotel.'

'Anybody touches me,' Raven warned, 'they're gonna get bit!'

Sheriff Cobb said, 'Now, now, girl, there'll be none of that. You just walk yourself out of here like Mr Moonlight says.'

'I'm not moving,' she said stubbornly. Then to Gabriel, 'Being a man means being responsible. Ain't that what you told me?'

'Don't matter what he told you,' Latigo said before Gabriel could answer. 'I'm calling him out and unless he's a yeller dog, he'll face me.'

Everyone held their breath.

All the air seemed to be sucked out of the cantina.

Gabriel smiled, wolfishly. 'Tomorrow,' he said to Latigo. 'On Silver . . . in front of the hotel.' Without waiting for a reply, he grabbed Raven by the arm and marched her outside.

CHAPTER THIRTY

As they crossed the busy dirt street to their hotel, avoiding buckboards, riders and freight-wagons, Raven begged Gabriel to change his mind.

'I can't,' he said grimly. 'Not even if I wanted to.'

'Why not?'

'You heard him.'

144

'So he called you yellow. So what? Words ... that's all they are.'

'Some words you can't walk away from.'

'Sure you can. You know you ain't yellow. I know you ain't yellow. So does everyone else – includin' Mr Rawlins. That's all that matters.' When he didn't reply, she added: 'Remember what Momma told you?'

' 'Bout what?'

'Posturing. How men had this silly gunfighter code they thought they had to follow, even if it meant dyin' for it. Remember that?'

He did but he didn't want to talk about it, so instead he said, 'How long were you listenin' outside?'

'Long enough to hear Sheriff Cobb say your ways are over. That men like you'n Mr Rawlins are standing in the way of progress and how sooner or later some dirty coward like Charley Ford would shoot you in the back.'

Gabriel didn't say anything. They had reached the opposite planked sidewalk now and, without breaking stride, he led her into the hotel and up to their room.

There, he stood silently looking out the window at the street below. Frustrated, Raven joined him.

'What're you doin', looking for a place to die?'

Angered by her sarcasm, he whirled and raised his hand as if to strike her. But as he looked into her upturned face, her large, expressive, dark eyes moist with tears, all his anger faded and he gently wrapped his arms around her and hugged her to him.

'Oh, G-Gabe,' she wept, 'I'm so scared. If something was to happen to you I ... I don't know what I'd do. I really don't.'

'Nothing's goin' to happen to me,' he assured her.

'But he's so fast ... you said so yourself.'

'I'm fast too.'

'I know, but ... what if he's faster?'

'That's somethin' I'm not worried about. You shouldn't be either. Tomorrow we got a train to catch to California. And after that, schoolin' and then . . . you got a hotel to buy an' me a rockin' chair, so I can sit an' spit all day . . . remember?'

Raven nodded and smiled through her tears. 'And a spittoon,' she said. 'So you don't mess up my front porch.' Suddenly she was sobbing.

Gabriel held her tightly, stroking her hair and trying to soothe her. But even as he spoke he felt the same icy hand gripping his jugular and deep inside himself he knew doubt for the first time.

What if Raven was right? What if he wasn't as fast as Latigo? But he was. Yes, but what if he wasn't? What if he really wasn't? What then?

Christ, there's a hell of a thought. *What then?*

CHAPTER THIRTY-ONE

Though it was two hours past midnight, Latigo Rawlins was still sitting with his boots propped up on the window ledge, drinking rye from a bottle he'd bought at the cantina, so the knock on his hotel room door didn't wake him.

But it did rattle him some. Grabbing one of his ivory-handled Colts, he went to the door and quietly asked who it was.

'It's me – Raven.'

'Who?'

'Raven Bjorkman. Open up, Mr Rawlins. I want to talk to you.'

Surprised, and wondering if it was some kind of trick, the

diminutive handsome gunfighter stood to one side of the door then opened it slightly.

Sure enough, Raven stood alone in the hall. In a plaid shirt hanging outside her Levi's, knee-high buckskin moccasins and with her short black hair blown wild by a night wind, she looked like an orphan Apache.

Yet there was something very appealing about her and Latigo decided not to turn her away. 'Little late for house calls, ain't it?'

'I had to wait till Gabe was asleep.' When Latigo continued to look suspiciously at her, she said: 'Surely a famous shootist like you isn't afraid of one little girl?'

He grinned, amused by her sass, and let her in. 'If Gabe sent you to beg for his life, missy, you're flat wastin' your time.'

'Why would he do that? Darn fool, he can't wait for tomorrow to come so he can gun you down in front of everybody.'

It wasn't the answer he expected. 'You sayin' Gabe doesn't know you're here?'

' 'Course not. He'd whip silly me if he did. That's why I couldn't come earlier.'

'If you're not here to beg, then what—?' Latigo broke off as it suddenly hit him why Raven had come. 'Why you little vixen. You know Gabe can't win tomorrow so you came here to flirt with me . . . to get me to take you in. That's it, isn't it?'

He went to touch her, only to jerk his hand back as she whipped out Gabriel's bone-handled skinning knife from under her shirt and flashed it at him.

'Try that again,' she warned, 'an' I'll gut you neck to gizzard.'

More surprised than alarmed, Latigo laughed and withdrew his hand.

'Forgive me, Miss Bjorkman. Obviously I misinterpreted your intentions.' Still amused, he holstered his six-gun, returned to his chair and took a swig of whiskey. 'Now whyn't you tell me why you're here.'

'To make you an offer – a thousand dollars if you'll ride out tonight.'

Latigo smirked. 'Buyin' me off, that it?'

'Call it what you like, Mr Rawlins. It's the same amount as the reward, only this way you don't have to fret about gettin' killed.'

'No chance of that happenin'. If there was you wouldn't be here, now would you?'

'I'm here,' Raven said, irked by his mocking tone, ''cause I don't want to see Gabe or you killed.'

'You're here,' Latigo corrected, ''cause you know – just like Gabe knows – I'm faster than him. Not by much. Maybe just a fraction of a second. But that fraction will determine the difference between who lives and who ends up face down in the dirt.'

'If you take my money, no one ends up in the dirt.'

'Sorry. Not interested.'

She frowned, puzzled. 'A thousand's a thousand. What difference does it make who pays you, Mr Rawlins?'

'Right now, plenty. This is somethin' that should've been settled a long time ago. You and Gabe are leaving town tomorrow. I don't take him down now, hell, I mightn't get another chance. Then no one will ever know for sure who's fastest.'

'Is that so important?'

'Damn right it is.'

'Why?'

' 'Cause that's how history will remember me.'

'History?'

'Yeah. As Sheriff Cobb keeps sayin', gunmen like Gabe an' me, we're the last of our kind. Once we're gone, the breed's extinct. That means folks are goin' to remember us. An' I don't want to be remembered as some fancy-dressed, sawed-off bounty hunter or killer, but as the fastest gun in the territory. Maybe the fastest anywhere.'

She saw how determined he was and that scared her. 'Please, Mr Rawlins, I'm begging you—'

He cut her off with an impatient wave. 'Save your breath, missy. We're done here.' Rising, he held the door open for her. 'Sweet dreams.'

Desperate, Raven said: 'What if I made it two thousand? Would you ride out then?'

'Not for five thousand.'

Raven sighed, defeated. 'I hope you rot in hell,' she said and stormed off.

'That,' Latigo called out after her, 'is a foregone conclusion.'

Gabriel was sitting on the bed, smoking in the dark, when she quietly opened the door of their hotel room and tiptoed inside. She saw him instantly and stopped, frozen, desperately trying to think of what to say.

'Did he agree?' Gabriel asked, not looking at her.

Startled by his question, Raven decided not to make things worse by lying and said, 'No.'

'Reckoned as much.'

'How'd you know where I went?'

He didn't answer. She watched the ash on his cigarette glow bright orange as he inhaled, then said, 'Are you awful angry with me?'

'Not angry so much as disappointed.'

'I only did it 'cause I love you. Don't want to lose you.'

'I know.'

Tinkling music from an upright saloon piano wafted in through the open window; followed by men and women laughing. Raven stood there, eyes downcast, utterly miserable.

'C'mere.' Gabriel patted the bed. Then as she sat beside him. 'I know you were just tryin' to help. But what you don't understand is by beggin' Latigo not to kill me, you proved you got no faith in me – me, the man your mother chose to look after you, to help you get all growed up. That's a hard pill to swallow.'

'But that's not true! I do have faith in you, Gabe. Lots an' lots of faith. Honest. And I know you'll always take good care of me.'

Again, the ash glowed brightly in the darkness.

'It's just that . . . I got to thinking . . . worrying about how somethin' might go wrong. I mean it could, you know. Things go wrong all the time. Someone could yell an' distract you just as you started to draw . . . or dirt could fly in your eye . . . you could even suddenly sneeze or get the hiccups . . . anything. An' then, no matter how fast you are, that'd give Mr Rawlins an edge and—'

'Latigo don't need an edge.'

'What do you mean?'

'He can clear leather faster than me.'

Horrified, she said, 'Then how can you beat him?'

'By shootin' straighter. Killing a man ain't just a matter of quick reflexes. Anyone who thinks that is already feet up. What's most important is makin' sure that your first shot counts; that the other fella's dead before he can get off a second shot an' this time maybe kill you.'

'B-But what if . . . the other fella's faster *and* he can shoot straight?'

'Then you never have to question yourself again.'

CHAPTER THIRTY-TWO

The next morning Gabriel awoke to find Raven cuddled against him on the floor. She was sound asleep. Her lovely pursed lips fluttered each time she breathed out. Touched by the realization that she'd gotten out of bed and joined him during the night, he leaned over and gently kissed her on the forehead.

She stirred in her sleep, one hand absently rubbing her brow as if brushing away a fly, but didn't awaken.

Gabriel smiled. My God, how much she meant to him!

He studied her for a long time, like a man trying to memorize something he might never see again; then he rose, dressed, stepped into his boots, grabbed his hat and gunbelt and quietly left the room.

Outside, dawn was breaking. The rising sun was the color of fresh-baked bread. As it crested the distant mountains its brightness outlined the craggy peaks and turned the dove-gray sky a pale, luminous gold.

But night wasn't giving up easily. Darkness clung to the town like a forbidding shroud. Usually the air was cool, crisp and dry; this morning a damp misty dew glistened on the rooftops, boardwalks and hitch-rails; while the ever-present wind off the desert not only spun the vanes of the windmills but gave the air a chilling bite.

Gabriel shivered. Pulling up the collar of his denim jacket he walked to the middle of the street. There he paused and looked about him. Was there anything he could do to give himself an edge against Latigo? Silver Avenue ran north and south, so he knew the sun wouldn't be a problem no matter which way he faced. Nor was he superstitious, having killed his enemies while facing all points of the compass. But remembering Raven's warning that dirt might blow in his eyes, he told himself to be sure to face south so that his back was to the wind.

One thing he knew he didn't have to worry about was a sniper hiding on the rooftops; perhaps on another day Latigo might have hedged his bet and hidden a rifleman up there, but not today. Today his reputation was at stake and such was

151

the handsome little gunfighter's ego that Gabriel knew it was all-important to him not to sully it, to kill his rival fair and square.

Los Gatos was not open for business at this early hour. But the front door was ajar and Gabriel pushed inside and saw someone working in the kitchen. It was the same lumpy middle-aged woman whom he'd previously spoken to regarding the man playing solitaire. Gabriel entered, bid her good morning in Spanish and asked if he could buy a cup of coffee.

The woman stopped kneading her tortilla dough, took a black iron pot from atop the stove and filled a mug with hot coffee. It was the color of tar and almost the same consistency. But to Gabriel it was nectar and he gave her a silver dollar. Grateful, she insisted on making him breakfast. He sat at a rickety little table opposite the stove and attacked a pile of eggs, beans, rice and tortillas. Normally, he would have easily wolfed everything down. But today, halfway through the meal he pushed the plate away. The woman anxiously asked him what was wrong. Not wanting to admit it was nerves he grimaced, rubbed his stomach and blamed his loss of appetite on too much tequila.

Outside, as he crossed over to the hotel, he tried to figure out why he was so nervous. He knew he wasn't afraid of dying. He'd already faced death on numerous occasions and never once been nervous. So why now?

Just then he happened to look up and saw Raven watching him from the window of their hotel room. She waved half-heartedly to him then turned away so he wouldn't see she was crying.

His heart went out to her. And suddenly, clearly, he knew why he was nervous. He was afraid he might lose her.

CHAPTER
THIRTY-THREE

By mid-morning the planked sidewalks lining both sides of Silver Avenue were jammed with people. The whole town knew about the impending gunfight and everyone wanted to tell their grandchildren they had witnessed it.

The boardwalks fronting *Los Gatos* and the Commercial Hotel were especially crowded. And those not standing outside were gathered in the windows of the stores and saloons, their faces pressed against the glass as they anxiously waited for noon to arrive.

Meanwhile, Sheriff Cobb, determined to prevent the ever-swelling crowd from getting out of hand, had sworn in six temporary deputies and instructed them to patrol Silver Avenue from Pine to Elm. Their orders were to disarm anyone carrying a gun or being disorderly, and to arrest all drunks. This severe action was to pacify the Mayor and the City Council who, the night before, had angrily questioned his motives for allowing a gunfight to take place in their peaceful community. Don't forget, he also reminded them, this gunplay would not only eliminate one or both of the last two dangerous gunmen in the territory but would eventually become part of the Deming folklore – like Billy the Kid's jailbreak in nearby Alamogordo – something every town needed if they wanted to lure rich Eastern tourists to the area.

About eleven-thirty, the local photographer, a gangly congenial young man from Kansas named Pete Weyborne, set up his camera and tripod in the street directly in front of the hotel. Though all the locals referred to his camera as a 'shutter-box,' it was actually a recent innovation from Kodak known as the 'B' Daylight model. It consisted of a simple black box, with a lens and string-shutter assembly that allowed the photographer to load and unload roll-film outside the darkroom – in daylight as the name suggested.

Pete was a perfectionist and to make sure he did not ruin this golden opportunity, as Sheriff Cobb had called it, he gave two boys a nickel each to act as stand-ins for the gunmen, and then for the next thirty minutes drove them crazy by moving his camera around, 'framing' them from different angles until he finally found the one that satisfied him.

Shortly before noon Raven sat watching the now-huge crowd from her hotel window. She had long ago cried herself out, and seemed to have accepted both the gunfight and Gabriel's possible death as inevitable. But the crowd and their ghoulish excitement at seeing two men shooting one another angered and disgusted her.

Turning to Gabriel, who sat smoking on the bed, she said: 'I hate them. They're like a bunch of buzzards. Laughing and joshin' around. Why, you'd think they were waitin' for a parade to go by, not to watch two people trying to kill each other.'

Gabriel didn't answer. Exhaling a smoke ring he watched it slowly drift upward and dissipate as it reached the ceiling. In his mind he saw himself with his father as they rode through a mountain pass in Colorado. Ahead, a crowd of people from a nearby town were gathered on a hillside overlooking a dangerous curve in the railroad tracks. Curious, his father had asked one man what was going on. Everyone was waiting for the gold camp special to go by, the man replied, adding that because of the long, steep grade sometimes the brakes gave out and the train jumped the tracks.

Horrified, the Reverend Moonlight began to berate the crowd. At first they ignored his ranting. But after a little they got angry and turned on him and young Gabriel had to drag his father away before the crowd beat him.

It was a lesson the teenager never forgot.

Five minutes before noon Gabriel buckled on his gunbelt, made sure his Colt was fully loaded then put on his hat and joined Raven at the window.

'I'll see you shortly,' he told her.

She nodded, but wouldn't look at him.

'Don't forget we got a train to catch in a couple of hours.'

Again she nodded; again she wouldn't look at him.

Gabriel had a million things to tell her but he couldn't make himself say them. Giving her a hug and a kiss on the top of her head, he left.

Raven felt her eyes burn but no tears came. Rising, she pulled the curtains shut and threw herself face down on the bed.

CHAPTER THIRTY-FOUR

A deputy with a shotgun was waiting for Gabriel when he emerged from the hotel. He ordered the crowd on the boardwalk to step back so Gabriel could pass and then escorted the gunman into the hot, sun-scorched street.

Sheriff Cobb, timepiece in hand, stood alone in the middle of Silver Avenue. He nodded at Gabriel and signaled to Weyborne to get ready to photograph the shootout.

Standing with his back to the south, Gabriel felt the wind

whipping against his legs. He looked around for Latigo. The fastidious little gunman was nowhere in sight.

'Where is he?' he asked the Sheriff.

'Still in the cantina. But he knows he's got to come out 'fore noon.'

Gabriel smiled to himself. Latigo had made his first mistake. If he was trying to rattle Gabriel, then he must feel he needed an edge, which meant he was not as sure of himself as he pretended. That was a good sign and Gabriel felt a wave of confidence spread through him.

He looked up at his hotel window. It was open but the curtains were drawn. He was thankful. He knew that Latigo's first bullet would hit him somewhere, but hopefully not fatally, and didn't want Raven to see him get shot.

'Twenty seconds,' Sheriff Cobb called out.

The batwing doors of *Los Gatos* swung open and Latigo stepped out into the brilliant sunlight. Second mistake, Gabriel thought. It was dark in the cantina and Latigo would need time for his eyes to get fully adjusted to the glare.

But if the El Paso gunman was worried about anything, he surely didn't show it. Tipping his hat to the excited crowd, he swaggered into the middle of the street.

Sheriff Cobb signaled for the crowd to be silent and then turned to Pete Weyborne. The young photographer nodded to show he was all set.

The sheriff looked at the two gunmen, 'Whenever you're ready, make your play, gents,' and stepped back out of the line of fire.

Gabriel and Latigo stared at each other. They were less than twenty paces apart and knew they wouldn't miss at that range. Both were poised to draw; both seemed reluctant to draw first.

Gabriel knew that Latigo, like most gunmen who wore two guns, would only draw one of them. He also remembered Latigo always rolled his smokes with his left hand, suggesting the little gunfighter was left-handed. So he concentrated on Latigo's left forearm, knowing it had to move before his hand did.

Another second dragged by. Then Gabriel saw something in Latigo's narrowed, amber eyes that told him the little gunfighter was about to slap leather.

Gabriel tensed, ready to grab his Colt – and at that instant a gust of wind blew. Dust swirled around his boots. Gabriel saw Latigo blink and knew dust had blown into his eyes. It was the edge he needed. His gun leapt into his hand, thumb cocking back the hammer. But in the split-second before Gabriel pulled the trigger he saw something glinting in the sunlight above Latigo's left shoulder. He knew, even before he actually looked, that it was a rifle poking out between the curtains in his hotel room window. It was aimed at Latigo and Gabriel knew it must be Raven, even though he couldn't see her.

'No!' he yelled. 'Don't!'

Latigo whirled, saw the rifle, jerked his gun and fired at the window – all in one fluid, blurring motion, everything happening so fast it was over before anyone realized what happened.

There was a sharp cry in the room. The rifle, Gabriel's Winchester, fell from the window and landed on the crowded boardwalk.

By then Gabriel was already running, elbowing his way through the startled onlookers and racing into the hotel.

Without slowing, he ran to the stairs, vaulted up them two at a time and raced along the landing to his room. Ramming the door open with his shoulder he burst inside and saw Raven lying limp and crumpled on her side below the window.

His heart froze. Dreading the truth, he kneeled beside her and gently rolled her over. She didn't move. He cradled her in his arms. Blood streamed from the bullet wound creasing her

157

temple and her big black eyes stared blankly at him.

Horrified, he pressed his ear against her chest and listened for a heart beat.

Nothing!

With a cry of anguish, he scooped up her limp body and ran from the room.

As he pounded down the stairs he saw Latigo and the sheriff entering the lobby. Behind them came a large, barrel-bellied man in a suit carrying a black bag. Following him were several deputies, shotguns held protectively in front of them as they tried to keep the crowd back.

'Set her down there,' Dr Carstairs said, indicating the sofa. Gabriel obeyed. The doctor pushed him aside, got out his stethoscope and pressed it against Raven's heart.

Dear God, Gabriel prayed, don't let her be dead.

A hand gripped his shoulder. He turned, saw Latigo looking at him. For the first time Gabriel saw sadness in the little gunfighter's amber eyes.

'I . . . I didn't know,' he said. 'I swear—'

'Will you people shut up!' Dr Carstairs said. The lobby went quiet. Dr Carstairs unbuttoned Raven's shirt and again pressed the stethoscope over her heart.

Gabriel held his breath. His world seemed to stop.

'She's alive,' Dr Carstairs said finally. He examined her wound and looked relieved. 'Lucky for her the bullet just grazed her skull. Any deeper and I'd be calling the undertaker.'

Gabriel could breathe again. 'Will she be all right, Doc?'

'Sure. Once she comes around she'll have a headache for a while, but otherwise she'll be fine.' He added, 'Somebody fetch me some hot water and a clean towel.'

'I'll do it,' the desk clerk said. He smiled sympathetically at Gabriel and hurried off.

CHAPTER THIRTY-FIVE

Less than two hours later Gabriel and Sheriff Cobb stood outside the Union Depot, sun hot on their backs, waiting for the train to California. Behind them a subdued Raven, head bandaged, sat quietly on a shady bench next to their carpetbags.

The sheriff gave her an anxious look. 'If you want to stay another night,' he told Gabriel, 'that's OK with me.'

'Thanks. But there's no point,' Gabriel said. 'Doc says she'll be fine. Said in a way the long train ride'll be good for her. Stop her from jumpin' around too much.'

The two men stood there sweating in silence.

'Funny how things work out,' Sheriff Cobb said.

Gabriel nodded. 'Sorry I ruined your memoirs.'

The sheriff grinned and ran his fingers through his cropped, iron-gray hair. 'You didn't. By the time I get around to puttin' what happened today on paper, it'll read like the stuff legends are made of.'

There was a distant train whistle. People around them began saying goodbye to their friends.

Sheriff Cobb offered Gabriel his hand. 'Good luck, son. Take care of that little gal.'

'With my life,' said Gabriel.

'Don't forget to buy a copy of my book when it's published.'

'Wouldn't miss it.'

'Oh, I almost forgot.' Sheriff Cobb pulled a folded note from his pocket and handed it to Gabriel. 'Latigo gave me this before he left town.'

Tipping his hat to Raven, who smiled, he walked to his roan, stepped into the saddle and rode off into town.

'What's it say?' Raven said, as she joined Gabriel.

He read the note. Chuckled.

'Well?' Raven demanded.

'Just men talk,' Gabriel said. 'Inappropriate for a lady.' Crumpling the note, he tossed it away. The wind caught it and sent it rolling along the railroad tracks like a miniature white tumbleweed.

The train whistle blew again, closer this time.

'Look,' pointed Raven. 'There she comes.'

Gabriel looked out across the flat, sun-baked land and saw smoke curling up on the horizon. As he did he felt Raven's fingers intertwine with his and he gave them a gentle squeeze.

Life, he realized, for once hadn't jumped up and bitten him.